"I can't go o[n] just staying here."

Luc smiled at her words. "Then I'll have to try to persuade you, Julia." he said. His lips caught hers, startling her for a moment. She was dazed when he lifted his head. Shame flooded her, and she lifted her hand to strike him, but he caught it and held it against his chest.

"So! Now we know, then, *mademoiselle*," he said softly. "I have overstepped the bounds of hospitality, but you needed that kiss as much as I!"

"Take me back!" Julia snapped as she sat bolt upright in the car. "If you ever touch me again, I'll go straight home, in spite of Justine!"

"I think not, Julia," he said quietly. "I told you that I would alter your life, did I not, though I didn't realize how very much. But we have not yet finished our discussion by any means."

PATRICIA WILSON used to live in Yorkshire, England, but with her children all grown up, she decided to give up her teaching position there and accompany her husband on an extended trip to Spain. Their travels are providing her with plenty of inspiration for her romance writing.

Books by Patricia Wilson

HARLEQUIN PRESENTS

HARLEQUIN ROMANCE

Don't miss any of our special offers. Write to us at the following address for information on our newest releases.

Harlequin Reader Service
901 Fuhrmann Blvd., P.O. Box 1397, Buffalo, NY 14240
Canadian address: P.O. Box 603,
Fort Erie, Ont. L2A 5X3

PATRICIA WILSON

the gathering darkness

Harlequin Books

TORONTO • NEW YORK • LONDON
AMSTERDAM • PARIS • SYDNEY • HAMBURG
STOCKHOLM • ATHENS • TOKYO • MILAN

Harlequin Presents first edition November 1989
ISBN 0-373-11221-1

Original hardcover edition published in 1988
by Mills & Boon Limited

CHAPTER ONE

IT WAS wonderful outside in the garden, and Julia stopped weeding to sit back on her heels for a moment, enjoying the sight of so much work come to fruition. They were lucky to have such a big garden so close to the city, lucky too to have such a big house, not that they needed it now.

Her eyes became sad, introspective, a state that she had thought she would be coming out of but from which she had never escaped.

'Oh, Lucy!'

Whispering the name aloud sometimes helped, so long as her father never heard. This time, though, her eyes swam with tears, her throat tightened with grief and the colours of the garden on a brilliant May afternoon faded to pale, ghostly shades, no longer important.

Three years, and the laughing face of Lucy still danced before her eyes. She would have been eleven now, her beloved little sister. Born so long after Julia, she had been a ray of sunshine in their lives, more precious still because, without her mother, Julia had taken on the role of mother herself. From fourteen years old she had shared the rearing of Lucy with her father and with Mrs Dobson, who had been their housekeeper for so long.

They would never be the same again, none of them. Her father was a different man, and even Mrs Dobson no longer sang around the house in her squeaky, off-

5

key voice. The sunlight had gone with Lucy. Maybe that was why Julia had fallen so easily under Graham's spell, believing him when he spoke of marriage, her love poured on to him when she should have seen him for what he was: ambitious, calculating and hard.

Her father was coming back across the wide lawn, the secateurs in his hand, and she knew he would sit down by her in the garden chair against the white table. Surreptitiously she dried her eyes, ready to smile brilliantly up at him as he joined her.

'What a glorious day for this time of the year!' He dropped into the seat, pulling off his gardening gloves, and her eyes followed the movement, seeing his hands emerge, square-fingered, clever, beautiful hands, the hands of a surgeon. The choking feeling rose again and she had to move, to pull off her own gloves, dust the loose soil from her jeans, make movement to gain time to recover.

'Everything looks splendid!' she said briskly. 'I see we're going to have plenty of blossoms on the lilac trees this year, they're well into bud.'

'Yes.' His eyes scanned the length of the garden, gazing over the lovely Old English setting they had made together, therapy to rid their hearts of pain. Sometimes it worked, but not too often.

It was so quiet, so slumberously still that they heard the chiming of the front door bell even from the garden, and Paul Redford glanced up at Julia.

'Expecting anyone, dear?' he asked quietly. They never mentioned Graham or his cruel desertion of her for a well-placed heiress, a woman who could certainly further his career. She knew that her father ignored him when they met in the hospital, and she knew too that it was fortunate that they were in different departments and in very different spheres. Doctor Graham Adams was important only to himself, small fry indeed in the world of Professor Paul Redford.

'There's a gentleman to see you, Professor!' Mrs Dobson appeared in the french window and walked across quickly, lowering her voice. 'I asked what his business was and I reminded him that it was Sunday, but he won't take no for an answer. I think he's foreign!' she finished in a whisper, her face showing that this explained all.

'Damn! I wish they wouldn't do this! Why can't the hospital deal with things like this at the proper time? I imagine it's one of those new students with some totally idiotic problem! Send him out here, Mrs Dobson!'

'Shall I go and...?' Julia began quietly, preparing to leave them to it. Her father did not like to be disturbed, and it usually took two or three weeks before this fact dawned on any new students.

'Stay here, Julia!' he ordered. 'We both look sufficiently relaxed to make it quite clear that we're off duty! You'll probably be able to answer all his questions, anyway, then I can get back to the roses!' he added with a chuckle.

She smiled and they both sat down, her father tall and distinguished-looking, his thick, white hair slightly untidy after an afternoon in the garden, Julia fair and slender, her rich, corn-coloured hair pulled back into a ponytail, her deep blue eyes large in her face, shadowed with grief not yet healed.

She was twenty-four but didn't look it at all. Her slender figure, the large, deep blue eyes that were now shadowed, the sweet sympathy of her mouth all belied her age. She looked sometimes no more than sixteen, Paul Redford thought. His poor, sweet Julia with the bright mind and a heart twice broken.

It was not a student, that much was instantly apparent. They both came slowly to their feet as the man stood at the french window, pausing to watch them for a moment. This was not a man who had come with some insignificant problem.

He was tall, athletic-looking, his skin deeply tanned, his hair black and heavy. There was an austere look on the handsome face, the look of a man who smiled rarely, and he radiated raw power even from there. The dark eyes took in the scene swiftly, but there was no apology on his ascetic face and Julia could see that none would be forthcoming. He was a man accustomed to being obeyed, and his attitude was not about to change for them.

There was an animal grace about him as he crossed the lawn that brought a quick shiver of fear racing down Julia's spine. He was trouble, she knew it, and the glittering gaze that flared over her only added to that certainty. He was lean, lithe, his movements alone telling of his utter self-assurance.

'Professor Redford?' After that one all-encompassing look, he ignored Julia and concentrated on her father, his gaze riveted on her father's fine face, his bright blue eyes. 'I am Luc Marchal!'

He paused, making no attempt to shake hands, his whole being dominant as if his very presence was a command.

'Sit down, please. Monsieur Marchal!' Suddenly, her father sounded weary, looked older and he motioned very tiredly to a seat opposite Julia. She sat too, slowly and uneasily. She had rarely seen her father look so defeated, not for three years. A dread grew in her then that had her staring at the Frenchman warily.

The cold, dark eyes swept over her pitilessly, a query in them: what was she doing here? The eyes said that plainly with no words spoken and in her consternation she almost rose, obeying an unspoken order.

'Please stay, Julia!' Her father was now seated, his old authority about him, the shock, whatever it had been, over, and Julia stayed, taking her cue from her father, her professional training coming to her rescue as she looked back into the dark, almost black eyes that had told her to leave.

'My daughter Julia, Monsieur Marchal,' her father said in an unbelievably stiff tone.

'Enchanté, mademoiselle.' He barely glanced at her, although he rose instantly and bowed in her direction. His eyes, though, were all for her father. Now that she had not obeyed his silent command to leave, he had dismissed her as unimportant. He looked as if courtesy was second nature to him, but it was barely there now. Whatever had brought him here was so consuming, so dear to his heart that the more pleasant things of life were not to be given more than a slight consideration.

'You know why I am here, Professor Redford!' he said incisively. 'We will not waste time on preliminaries!'

'I know why you're here, Monsieur Marchal,' her father agreed with a severe look at him. 'I have answered all your letters personally because I have the greatest sympathy with you, but the answer is, and will always be, no!'

'The child will die, professor! I cannot see how your great sympathy will prevent that!'

There was a vibrant force about the Frenchman's voice that held Julia spellbound, although every instinct urged her to be outraged at the way he had spoken to her father. The lean, deeply tanned face was alive with scorn, the black, glittering eyes punishingly intent.

To her astonishment she saw a deep flare of red cross her father's face. He was angry, angrier than she had ever seen him.

'You have come here, uninvited, disturbing both myself and my daughter, Monsieur Marchal,' he said bitingly. 'I have given you my answer and it is final. I will not accept the child as a patient!'

'Because she is French, Professor Redford? Is this why you, the best neuro-surgeon in two continents, refuse to save the life of a child of eight years old?'

'Oh, no!' Julia's cry brought the dark eyes round to her, surprise in them as she jumped to her feet, shaken to her very core.

'Julia, my dear girl!' Her father crossed to her as she turned to leave, his arms tightening round her. She was on the very edge of tears and unwilling to give way to her feelings before this arrogant Frenchman. 'My dear, don't upset yourself.'

Her father was bitterly angry, although pale himself, and Luc Marchal too was on his feet, consternation on his face, utter bewilderment at this sudden little scene.

'*Mademoiselle,*' he began softly, 'if my words have upset you...'

'They have, Monsieur Marchal!' her father said vehemently, urging Julia to her seat and sitting in the chair beside her, keeping her hand in his as she sat white-faced. 'Since you are not content to take no for an answer, since you have stormed your way into my house demanding an explanation when I have already told you that I no longer perform operations and that I work now merely in a teaching capacity, I will give you the explanation that you demand.

'I have not operated for three years. The last patient died under my hands. That patient too was a child, a little girl of eight years old. I will never operate again!'

'You are not the only surgeon to lose a patient, Professor,' Luc Marchal said quietly. 'Others have done it before you and since. They still use their skills to save others.'

'But I do *not*!' Her father stood, his breathing agitated, pain in his eyes that was hidden by cold rage. 'The child, *monsieur*, was mine! My Lucy! Julia's sister!'

He turned and walked stiffly away, entering the house, leaving them without a backward glance, and Julia stared at Luc Marchal, her eyes accusing.

'*Mademoiselle!* How can I tell you how much I regret this? In my own pain, I would not wish to bring pain to others. How could I possibly have known? In his letters, he gave no explanation. He simply refused!' He shrugged in disgust. 'I suppose that I am too accustomed to people offering explanations to me.'

'It—it's all right,' she said quietly, taking a deep, steadying breath. 'You couldn't possibly have known. He—we never talk about it.' She raised deep blue eyes to his, eyes that still glittering with suppressed tears. 'Is—is the child a relative?' she asked tremulously.

'Yes,' he said flatly, a bleak, far-away look in his eyes. 'She is my niece. My brother is dead. She is all that is left of Jules!'

'What is her name?' Julia asked softly.

'Justine,' he said, his voice harsh with pain. 'She is eight years old, lively, dark and just a little wild.'

'You're describing my sister,' she whispered. 'Lucy was just like that.' She turned away abruptly. 'I'll see you out, Monsieur Marchal. I must go to my father.'

He followed her, saying nothing more until they stood at the opened front door.

'I was certain that I could get your father to help, to do the necessary operation,' he confessed quietly. 'All that I have succeeded in doing is to bring unhappiness to more than myself.'

'Perhaps when you get back to her in France, Monsieur Marchal, some French surgeon will be able to save her.'

He looked down at her steadily.

'I do not think that there is now time, *mademoiselle*,' he informed her. 'Justine is no longer in France. I brought her to England this morning. She is now in a private room at your father's hospital. I staked everything upon his help.'

'Oh! I'm so sorry!'

His lips twisted into a bitter smile. 'You are kind, but compassion will not save Justine. She needs your father's skill. Forgive me for the unhappiness I have brought to you, *mademoiselle*,' he said coldly. 'Goodbye.'

Julia watched him walk down the path and then shut the door firmly. She could not fail to feel sympathy but he was a hard man, unreachable. Inadvertently, she shuddered. He was like a man with secrets, dark secrets. There was a brooding air about him that was frightening. She hurried to her father, knowing that the old, old wound was re-opened.

It was a relief to get back to the hospital the next day. She felt uneasy about her father but there was nothing that he would allow her to say. From the moment that he had left her in the garden, he had shut himself in his room and answered only briefly when she had gone to him. He was back in the past again, burdened with guilt and grief, the outburst at the Frenchman rocking him so badly that he had no time even for Julia. It would all have to die down again.

'Anything new?' She took over from the night sister and stopped for the usual small but necessary conference.

'Mrs Brown is going out today after Mr Elton has done his rounds. Young Cynthia is allowed up for two hours this morning, no walking, though! Oh, yes, and Mrs Watkins is as troublesome as usual.'

Sister Todd smiled broadly and found an answering smile on Julia's face.

'This place will be very quiet when she goes home,' Julia remarked, straightening her cap and fastening her watch to her stiff, white apron. She looked very different today, another person entirely. The long, thick corn-coloured hair was swept up and pulled tightly back from her face, the frilled white cap set on top at a very straight and exact angle, and although her dark blue uniform dress made her look even more slender, she was seriously professional, Sister Redford, about to take the Woman's Surgical ward into her care.

'Better get off to bed, Jean,' she said softly. 'You look tired.'

'Yes,' Jean Todd sighed and chewed at her bottom lip. 'We've had quite a night. I'm afraid that I've saved the worst news until last, Julia. There's a patient in one of the private wards, a little French girl, head injuries. She's drifting in and out of a coma. Mr Elton is going to operate tomorrow as your father...as Professor Redford...'

She trailed away into unhappy silence and Julia patted her arm.

'It's all right, Jean. I know about the little girl. I'll go to see her as soon as I've done the rounds of the ward.'

'Her father was furious! He didn't take to Mr Elton. I thought he was going to refuse...but after all, he brought her all the way here on the off-chance.'

'Monsieur Marchal is the child's uncle,' Julia said quietly. 'He called on us yesterday.'

'Gosh! I'm sorry, Julia. I mean you've got enough on your plate right now, what with... Oh, God! Look, I'm going! Everything I say makes things worse. I can't seem to get control of my tongue. Put it down to the rotten night we've had.'

'Don't worry.' Julia made a quick dismissive gesture. She knew what Jean had been about to say. Everyone in the hospital knew that her engagement with Graham was off. It had happened so quickly that it was quite spectacular. Her mind flashed back to that evening a month ago. The ridiculous scene.

'Graham, I saw you with a lovely girl this afternoon. Who on earth was she?' She had not been too curious. It was not in her nature to be jealous and she had expected some laughing reply, not the serious reply she had received. It was the girl he was going to marry, a girl with a very wealthy father who wouldn't at all mind setting Graham up in a private practice if that was what Gloria wanted, and Gloria did!

'Are you all right?' Sister Todd touched her arm and Julia pulled herself back to the present.

'Of course! I was just thinking about the day. It's going to be busy.'

'It is! I'd better let you get started. I hope I haven't upset you, Julia.'

'You haven't.' Julia said firmly, giving her cap one final twitch. Upset! She sometimes felt that she was storing up a mental breakdown, hiding it away to take out later. Soon, though, she would be free from St Andrew's. She had handed in her resignation and now she was counting the time.

'Sister Redford! Thank God you're on duty again!' Mrs Watkins' shrill little voice echoed through the ward as soon as Julia stepped through the swing doors, and the staff nurse gave her a wry smile.

'Shall we go down to her straight off, Sister, and put ourselves out of our misery?' she asked with a grimace.

'We shall not, Staff! She can wait her turn.' Julia went from bed to bed, speaking to each patient in turn, checking their charts, finally fetching up against the invariably untidy bed of Mrs Watkins.

'I want you to speak to the doctor today, Sister Redford. I intend to go home tomorrow at the latest!'

'Your leg isn't healed yet, Mrs Watkins,' Julia said quietly, nodding to the staff nurse who went around the other side of the bed. Together they began to straighten the bedcovers.

'Look at you!' Mrs Watkins squeaked. 'More interested in the bed than the patient! What's so important about a tidy bed?'

'Not a lot!' Julia said in a matter-of-fact voice. 'It's good for the morale though, yours and ours. If we all look as tidy and pretty as possible, the day takes on a different outlook. In your case too, it tells me at a glance if you've been sneaking out of bed! Unless you keep off that leg, it will never heal. We're too short-staffed to watch you all the time. You have to take some responsibility for your own health, you know!'

'Well, I don't mind for you, but I'd do nothing at all for her,' Mrs Watkins grumbled, eyeing the staff nurse bitterly. 'She's rough!'

'The moment we're off the ward, I'll reprimand her,' Julia said seriously, her eyes twinkling at the staff nurse as they turned away.

'Right! I'll just keep still then!' Mrs Watkins said in a satisfied voice.

'I'll go out into the corridor and scream a bit,' the staff nurse whispered with a grin.

'Anything to keep her in bed!' Julia murmured. 'At this rate, she'll be here for ever.'

She walked back to the office, measuring out the morning's medication and handing the list to the staff nurse. Then she was alone. She was putting it off. She knew that. But it had to be faced. Quietly, her soft-soled shoes making no sound, she walked down the corridor to the side ward that held their only private patient, a little girl with dark hair, an eight-year-old child who was sometimes a little wild.

A nurse was standing outside the room, looking distinctly worried, clearly torn between conflicting orders.

'What's wrong, Nurse James?' Julia stopped beside her, her deep blue eyes keenly alert.

'I'm supposed to stay with the little French girl, Sister Redford, report any change, but the man came in and told me to wait outside. I didn't quite know what to do.' She was very young and anxious and Julia nodded.

'Go and put the kettle on in the office. I'll call you back in a minute.' She knew who was in the room and she knew that he was too much for Nurse James, too much for her too, but she had the responsibility now. She straightened her back and walked in.

Luc Marchal was sitting beside the bed, his strong, tanned figure gently holding the pale hand of the child who lay there unmoving, and at the sound of the door he spun round angrily, no doubt expecting to see the young nurse who had been despatched as being unnecessary. At the sight of Julia, he stood slowly and she thought that she had never seen such a stunned expression on any face in her life.

'Mademoiselle Redford?' His dark eyes swept over her, examining her in detail from her severely tidy hair and her white frilled cap to her dark blue uniform and white apron. 'Sister Redford?' he asked in astonishment. 'But you are a young girl, little more than a child!'

'Twenty-four, Monsieur Marchal,' she said stiffly, unprepared for the wave of tingling shock that hit her as his eyes held hers. 'I assure you that I am qualified and in charge of the ward for the day. My authority includes this room, and you had no right to dismiss the nurse who was here!'

'She was unnecessary at the moment,' he assured her, his mind still not quite on the subject, otherwise he would never have allowed her to speak like that, she was sure. 'In any case, this is a private room!' he added sharply, coming back to the present with a snap.

'But still under my care, *monsieur*!' she returned as sharply, walking to the bed and looking down at the child.

It took all her courage and only after a deep breath dared she focus her eyes on the little face. It was lifeless, the closed eyes shadowed with blue, the pale cheeks like death. Automatically she took the child's pulse. It was faint, barely there at all.

'How long has she been like this?' she asked sharply, reaching for the equipment on the side table and beginning to take a reading of the child's blood-pressure.

'As she is now? Since this morning!' he said tightly. 'Until then, she drifted in and out of consciousness but she did not know me. After the accident she seemed to be perfectly all right. It seemed that she had escaped from the crash that killed her parents without any more injury than a few scratches. Later she began to behave strangely, and soon she complained that her arm would not move. X-rays showed nothing, but finally they found it.'

'Pressure on the brain,' Julia said quietly, her face concerned at the child's blood-pressure.

'Yes!' His voice was harsh but she ignored him totally, her hand reaching for the chart at the foot of the bed, reading all the signs. Since she had taken over such a short time ago, the child had deteriorated rapidly. Before tomorrow's planned operation, this child would be dead. More than that, Derrick Elton did not have the supreme skills of her father.

She walked to the door and found Nurse James hovering again.

'Go on the ward, Nurse James, and stay there,' she ordered. 'Send the staff nurse here and tell her to wait for me, *inside* the room!'

'Yes, Sister Redford!' The little nurse almost ran and Julia turned along the corridor. By now her father would be in the hospital, he had a lecture at nine and he would have to leave it!

Julia came back fifteen minutes later with a porter and a trolley in tow and the door of the private room was wide open. So were Luc Marchal's dark eyes.

'Mademoiselle!' he began heatedly, his glare leaving the staff nurse who held her position by the bed with a stubborn expression that Julia knew well.

'Sister!' Julia corrected sharply. If she was to have trouble then she had better stand on her dignity. 'Will you please wait outside, Monsieur Marchal! You may use the office at the end of the corridor.' She turned away, dismissing him. 'Right, staff, let's get this patient ready for the theatre.'

'*Mademoiselle*—Sister Redford!' he said tersely. 'It is to be tomorrow, this operation. By then I may get your father to... I do not have great faith in this Monsieur Elton!'

'Mr Elton is a very fine surgeon!' Julia rounded on him in her most professional manner. 'However, he is not doing this operation.'

'Your father...?' he began in a taut voice, some small hope at the back of his eyes.

'Professor Redford will operate as soon as we can get your niece to the theatre, Monsieur Marchal,' Julia said firmly. 'Therefore, the sooner you obey my instructions and leave, the better it will be!'

A slow smile lit the dark contours of his austere face and he took her hand.

'Thank you, Sister Redford!' he said in a quiet, almost humble voice. 'You have persuaded him. I will never cease to be grateful.'

'He is not God, *monsieur*!' she warned him quietly, her hand tingling with the shock of contact with those hard, warm fingers. 'She is very, very ill.'

'I am aware of it,' he confessed, his dark eyes intent on her face. 'At the moment, though, he is the nearest thing to God that I have to hand, and you are an angel, a beautiful, severe and efficient angel sent to help Justine. Whatever you tell me to do, I will do it!'

'Simply wait in the office, Monsieur Marchal, and let us do what we are trained to do,' she answered stiffly.

'I obey, Sister Redford,' he said quietly as he kissed her hand. He left at once and Julia's astonished eyes met the equally stunned gaze of the staff nurse. There was no time to stand and gasp though, the small, pale face on the white pillows held all her attention.

'Right!' She moved forward and they worked in unison, well used to each other, each respecting the other's abilities.

Later, as the theatre trolley was wheeled away down the corridor, the staff nurse walking beside it, Julia turned and made her way back to the office, pausing at the open door to speak to a nurse.

'Strip the bed in the private room, Nurse,' she ordered, and then walked in to face the Frenchman.

'I saw them take her away!' he said tautly. 'You are not going with her?'

'I'm not a theatre sister, *monsieur*,' she explained wearily. 'Please sit down and you can have a cup of tea with me.'

'I want... I would like you to be with her,' he said harshly, still standing. Julia sat anyway and looked up at his great height, her deep blue eyes calm and firm all at the same time, although it took an effort.

'I am not trained for the theatre,' she told him quietly. 'I would only be in the way. When she comes back, I can help then.'

'How can you?' he said bitterly. 'She will be only one of many. You have a whole roomful of patients and Justine will get only her share of your attention! How can you be here and in her room at the same time?'

Julia sighed and stood, pulling back a curtain against her desk, indicating a small room there and the bed in it, the equipment by the walls.

'Your niece will be in the Intensive Care ward, Monsieur Marchal. My eyes will be on her for most of the time. I will be nursing her throughout each day. It is what I do best. Now please sit down.'

She handed him a cup of tea and he took it with a moody look on his face, his dark eyes meeting hers and holding her gaze.

'What do you think of her chances?' he said tightly.

'I can only tell you that my father is the best,' she said quietly. She tore her gaze away, looking out into the ward, knowing that soon she would have to go out there and smile. 'If—if she dies . . . I think it will kill my father. I don't imagine he can face that again and she's so like—like Lucy.'

'And yet it was you who persuaded him,' he reminded her softly.

'For two reasons,' she said, her white teeth sinking into her lower lip, her eyes far away, seeing the past. 'Your niece needed him and in many ways, he needed her; no other person would have done. If she lives, I think he will go back to doing what he was intended to do, saving lives. If she dies . . .'

She couldn't finish and he looked at her intently.

'You have a great amount of courage and compassion,' he said softly. 'It shows in your mouth, in your eyes. Yesterday, I did not even know that you existed. Now, though, I think that whatever happens, I have changed your life.'

A cold fear seemed to come from nowhere and race down her spine and it took all her professional training to keep her face bland. Even so, she was not at all sure that he did not know of her sharp shock of fear. His dark eyes were mercilessly intent and she stood to go on to the ward.

'It will take some time, Monsieur Marchal,' she said briskly, 'and I am very busy. If you would like to ring in about three hours, I may have some news for you.'

He nodded. 'I may ring you personally, Sister Redford?'

'Yes. Now, if you will excuse me...'

'I will return to my hotel. I would not wish to get in your way. Thank you for your help and for your kindness.'

He gave her that stiff little bow and suddenly he looked quite alien; she had not noticed that before. He was a dark and silent man and, she thought, dangerous. It was just a feeling, but right then it was overwhelming. She did not want him to change her life. She did not want him in her life. He had made so much of her actions, but she would have done the same for anyone. In this case, though, she was left with the frightening feeling that it gave him some hold over her, like an old saying, 'You have saved my life, therefore you are responsible for it.'

He had been angry that she had not been accompanying Justine to the theatre, jealous that her time would be shared with other patients. Only the sight of the room so close to her desk had silenced him. Julia watched him walk away, so tall and dark, so quietly masculine, but there was aggression there too, she already knew that. It was just below the surface waiting to erupt. If this operation failed...

She straightened her apron and hurried on to the ward. Only hard work would keep her mind away from the theatre, her father and the small child in his clever hands.

It would also rid her mind of the uneasy pictures that she was beginning to build around Luc Marchal.

Her father came along to see her later, and the brilliance of his blue eyes told her all that she wanted to know.

'Oh, Daddy! How is she?' she cried breathlessly, pulling him into the office and closing the door.

'She'll do! She's on her way up. It's over to you now, darling.' He hugged her close. 'Maybe now I can learn to live again,' he said quietly. 'Maybe I needed this to pull me back to the living, to my other daughter. Thank you, Julia, you have more courage than I.'

There were still tears in her eyes when Luc Marchal telephoned, but they were tears of happiness.

'Sister Redford?' he asked in a taut voice, and her whole being went out to him.

'I've got her here, *monsieur*!' she said happily. 'I can see her from where I'm standing. Of course, she's still sedated so tomorrow...'

'I may see her now?' he asked urgently. 'You will allow me?' Suddenly she was laughing, happiness welling up inside her.

'You can come to my office and look at her through the window. You can break every rule. If anyone questions you, I'll throw a tantrum!'

'I do not quite know what a tantrum is,' he confessed with a low laugh, 'but if you throw it then I am sure it will be severe, especially if you look as you did this morning when I sent out your nurse. I will be with you in twenty minutes, Sister Redford, and I will be on my very best behaviour.'

She put the phone down and for the first time in a very long time, she was laughing quietly.

CHAPTER TWO

HE CAME quickly after the call and stayed with Julia in the office, simply gazing with vibrant face upon Justine. There was nothing to see beyond the small, white face, the tightly bandaged head, but he barely took his eyes from her. There was now nothing of the light-hearted air about him that had come across on the telephone. He was silent, sombre, his face turned with unnatural intensity towards his niece.

'You will guard her well, Sister Redford?' he asked quietly, his eyes skimming briefly to Julia's face.

'She is my patient, Monsieur Marchal,' she said simply, but the vehemence of his reaction startled her.

'Justine must be more than that to you, *mademoiselle*! She has suffered enough. It is not enough that she lives! She must be happy, secure, untroubled by doubt!'

'Most of those things I can promise while she is in my care, Monsieur Marchal!' Julia said stiffly. 'Happiness is something that cannot be guaranteed, although I shall do my best.'

He turned completely to look at her, leaning against the desk, his arms folded, his elegantly clad legs crossed.

'While she is with you, she is safe,' he said, watching her face almost aggressively. 'I could wish that you were with her all the time, although I know that you would be less than efficient if you were to be here constantly.'

'I'm grateful to be allowed time off for good be-haviour!' Julia said wryly, adding as he continued to gaze at her, 'The night sister is very good, and for most of the time the child will be asleep. I take over every morning.'

'And what about your days off?'

'We're short-staffed,' Julia said quietly, her eyes turning to the small and rather tragic figure in the bed. 'While she is like this, I could arrange to be here every day; nobody would object, I imagine.'

'*Merci, mademoiselle*—er—Sister,' he said deeply, correcting his error with one of his rare smiles. His dark head tilted thoughtfully as he watched. 'I never expected that my gratitude would run so deeply with an English girl.'

'My duty, *monsieur*,' she said, a trifle coolly. His intent looks were beginning to worry her. Unless she was careful, this man and child, this odd pair, were going to invade her life. Some instinct warned her and her re-action was swift and guarded. She needed no further upset in her life.

'It was not your duty to persuade your father, Sister Redford,' he reminded her quietly.

'I had no other course of action, and in any case, he's glad. I think that we are both satisfied by the outcome, *monsieur*. Now, if you don't mind, I must ask you to leave. I have to get ready to hand over to the night sister.'

It was not merely her natural reaction to an intrusion into the quiet and carefully controlled running of the ward; she felt as if she was actually holding down some-thing powerful here. True, he was an anxious relative, but she had seen plenty of those, and reactions after a successful operation were usually very different from this. He had not relaxed at all. After that first burst of gladness, he was back to normal, if it was normal for him; he was back to a watchfulness that left her feeling very uneasy, as if they would all have to walk carefully.

He left unwillingly enough though, clearly not wanting to be the one to jeopardise his niece's chances in any way. As he left, Graham came round to the office door and Luc Marchal's dark eyebrows rose questioningly at the suddenly changed expression on Julia's face, her eyes cold and aloof.

'A doctor,' he murmured, seeing the white coat, the stethoscope in Graham's pocket. 'I hope that you will not be in any trouble for allowing me here, Sister Redford?'

'Don't worry!' Julia said tightly and unwisely, almost forgetting him in the way her bitterness flooded to the surface at the sight of Graham. 'He doesn't have the authority! This is *my* ward until I hand it over to Sister Todd.'

'Then I will bid you goodnight, Sister. I shall be here tomorrow.'

He left as Graham came to the door and Julia stepped outside with him. She had no intention of being trapped in the office by Graham Adams.

'Did you want something, Doctor Adams?' she said coldly as the Frenchman walked off down the shining corridor.

'Oh, for God's sake, Julia! Don't be like this, darling!' Graham attempted to take her hand and she stiffened into an almost military stance, her head high and rigid, her hand snatched away from his questing fingers.

'I'm very busy, Doctor Adams,' she bit out more loudly than she intended. 'If this is a social visit then please leave the ward!'

Graham growled under his breath but he could see that she was unyielding, and turning on his heel, he stalked off along the corridor that ran at right angles to the main one. Julia leaned against the door, her stiffly held shoulders falling, her face defeated. It was all right to let herself know, but nobody else. It had been a cruel blow when Graham had so easily tossed her aside for wealth and a possible future of power. She had no doubt that he would rise rapidly. He trampled to the top, standing on anyone who got in his way. She carefully wiped away the bitter tears that had flooded to her eyes.

Only then did she see that the Frenchman was still there, part way along the main corridor, his dark eyes vividly on her, his lean face full of unspoken questions.

'Sister Redford?' he said quietly, taking a step back towards her, but she turned quickly and went on to the ward. Right now she did not wish to be reminded that any self-concern on her part would jeopardise his niece's welfare, and she had no doubt whatever that he had been about to come back and say as much.

She was very pleased when her duty ended. It had been a very trying day, filled with dreads and high points, ending on a very sour note indeed with Graham's arrival and the Frenchman's domineering attitude. She wanted to get back to her father and share with him the joy of his achievement, to see his face at last back to that quiet happiness that she had seen for most of her life. She swung her red-lined cape over her shoulders and walked through the main doors of the hospital, down the wide steps.

Graham was waiting for her, pouncing on her before she could turn away.

'Julia, I've got to talk to you! I have to get you to myself for a while!' He took her arm but she snatched it away, turning on him furiously.

'How dare you accost me here, where anyone can see?' she raged quietly. 'How dare you speak to me at all after what you've done?'

'I still love you, Julia,' he said miserably. 'Do you know what it does to me seeing you every day and wanting you in my arms? Nothing has changed with me.'

'Oh, but it has!' she said bitterly and angrily. 'You're now engaged to another woman! You're set up for life I should think, certainly you're going to be married.'

'You don't know what she's like,' he muttered, his face flushed with frustration. 'I never intended it to happen. She's very persuasive. I've got to think of the future, though. I haven't got a famous surgeon for a father!'

'And neither had my father!' Julia snapped, her eyes filled with tears of anger and shame. 'He worked for his success, he didn't sell himself for it!'

'Julia!' His hand came back to her arm as he saw her tears, but it fell away rapidly at the sound of the cool voice that startled Julia into actually jumping, her face flushed with embarrassment, her tears quickly blinked away.

'Ah, you are here at last! I thought that you would never arrive. My car is over here.'

Luc Marchal appeared from nowhere and seemed to be towering over them, clearly aware of the atmosphere that stretched so painfully between them. He took Julia's arm firmly, turning her away from Graham and leading her across the road to his car.

'You do not have your own car at the hospital, *mademoiselle*?' he enquired softly.

'No, it's not worth the effort of getting it out; I usually get the bus.' She realised that she was shaking, and he must have felt it because his grip on her arm tightened. 'I'll get the bus now, if you don't mind,' she added stiffly.

'I will take you home,' he said quietly, opening the car door for her, and she was too shattered to refuse; in any case, Graham was still standing there, looking daggers at the Frenchman but unable to intervene.

'You—you weren't really waiting for me, were you?' she managed tremulously as he drove away, not even glancing at the angry figure of Graham Adams.

'Actually, I was,' he assured her. 'I could not help but see that you were upset at your encounter with that particular doctor in the hospital, although I did note that he obeyed your orders as everyone else seems to do. He was waiting outside, however, and I assumed that he waited for you.'

'Thank you, *monsieur*, but I don't need protection from hospital staff,' Julia said tightly. 'Nor do I usually accept lifts from relatives of my patients.'

'It is merely because of your patient that I am here, *mademoiselle*,' he replied with equal stiffness. 'I do not wish you to be upset! I wish for your complete tranquillity at this time. I have been making a few enquiries

about you and I am given to understand that you are a
very brilliant nurse; that is why you are in such a high
position so early in your life, or so they tell me. They
also tell me that your fiancé abandoned you for a girl
with—better prospects. If he is now to come back every
time he realises that there is much more to a woman
than money, then you will be unsettled almost constantly.
I do not intend to stand by and see that happen!'

'How *dare* you?' Julia took a full three seconds to
follow the lengthy speech and to get her breath back at
this high-handed interference. 'How dare you pry into
my private life and step into something that does not
concern you in the least?'

'While Justine is in your care,' he bit out angrily, 'you
have no private life as far as I am concerned. Already
you have saved her life!'

'My father did that, and . . .' Julia began heatedly, but
he would not allow her to continue.

'She was almost gone! I saw your face when you came
to her room and first looked at her. The other sister had
not long since handed over to you, and she had been
content to allow Justine to go on as before. She did not
see what you saw. You acted swiftly, courageously and
skilfully! *You* saved her! Your father was merely the in-
strument you called to your aid. As far as I am concerned, you are the best and Justine needs the best. I
will protect you from upset even if it means that I must
follow you, collect you and deliver you to the hospital
and physically restrain that doctor! I will not allow anything or anybody to come between you and Justine!'

Julia was speechless. Never in her whole life had
anyone behaved like this towards her, or regarded her

so highly that others were counted as mere secondary considerations of no concern. She had recognised trouble as soon as she had seen Monsieur Marchal, but what trouble she had envisaged she was not sure. It had certainly not been this, though!

'Monsieur Marchal,' she began softly, her manner careful in face of his obvious belief in his own towering capabilities. 'You must not take this attitude, and I assure you that...'

'Do not address me as if I were a lunatic, *mademoiselle*,' he advised sharply. 'My world revolves around one small girl at the moment, and I intend to take her back to France cured, healthy and happy. Anyone who steps between me and that desire will be thrust aside! You are necessary for her existence, responsible for the fact that she is alive at this moment. I intend to deal very severely with anyone who harasses you!'

'I am only a nurse, *monsieur*,' Julia said with growing exasperation.

'You are Justine's nurse!' he corrected fiercely, his dark face turned to her for a second with a look that silenced her. 'Until she is better, you are under my wing, Sister Redford, whether you wish to be or not. I intend to watch you, and to watch also those who would presume to interfere!'

It was quite hopeless, she conceded in astonishment. She could give him a good shaking, but he seemed quite capable of putting her across his knee and spanking her and then telling her to go to bed so that she would be alert to take care of Justine tomorrow. As to being harassed, she felt totally frustrated at this unbelievable attitude. Graham had receded into the very back of her mind. She was hovering between wild rage and wild laughter.

'It may not have dawned on you, Monsieur Marchal,' she informed him quietly, 'but you are harassing me yourself. My only intention tonight was to go home to my father and have a meal with him as we discussed Justine and her medical problems.'

'Excellent!' he said in a satisfied voice. 'You are an admirable nurse, Sister Redford! It is a miracle that Justine has found you. Do not worry, I will have you home long before you could have been there by bus.'

'The bus driver would not, however, have waded in to control my life!' Julia snapped irritably, quite sure that this had gone on long enough. 'Here we are!' she added sharply as her house came in sight. 'I shall not require you to take me to work tomorrow, *monsieur*. I invariably go with my father. Tomorrow night, I will make my own way home, deal with my own problems and ward off any unsuitable intruders in my own inimitable way. Goodnight!'

'I would like it very much if you and your father would dine with me tonight,' he said pleasantly, quite ignoring her anger.

'I assure you, *monsieur*, that *we* would not like it at all!' she bit out, turning away. 'I know I can answer for both of us in that. We have had a very trying day and I have had a very irritating ride home. Once again, *monsieur*, goodnight!'

He seemed to find it all suddenly amusing, but Julia did not. She decided though that her father could do without this amazing tale, and after a few deep breaths she went in, a smile on her face that matched the smile on his. It was a very happy evening, even though the thought of Monsieur Marchal did intrude several times as she found herself remembering his astonishing attitude. As an experience, she could have managed very well without it.

Luc Marchal seemed to be constantly at the hospital both to keep his eye on his niece's progress and to make quite sure that Julia was toeing the line. It was not at all pleasing. Justine's condition was quite normal for anyone who had undergone this type of surgery. She was dazed, almost unmoving, and although she clearly recognised her uncle, she made no effort to speak or to make any contact with him.

Most days he left the hospital with a deep frown on his dark face. The only time his expression lightened was when he came in unexpectedly once or twice to find Julia sitting beside the child's bed, her hand clasping the frail little fingers, her voice quiet and soothing as she talked. Justine never made any attempt to reply, but eventually the dark eyes became intent, amusement in their black depths as Julia told her some of the funny stories that she had once told Lucy. Justine never laughed aloud, though, not even after many days of contact.

Physically, the child's progress was excellent, and Paul Redford saw her daily, sometimes more than once. He had returned to his life's work and the whole hospital seemed to rejoice about it. Even so, Justine was his special case, his talisman, and Julia could see that she puzzled him. Justine was now sitting up, taking her meals with no problem, medication down to a minimum, but she had made not one sound, no laughter, no tears, not one single word.

'She can't speak, can she?' Julia said to her father one afternoon when he had visited the child and then come worriedly into the office. 'What went wrong?'

'Nothing at all, darling!' Paul Redford said in a puzzled voice. 'We've had her back down for tests and X-rays, as you know, and there is nothing whatever to account for this, no motor damage at all. I assume there was nothing wrong with her before this accident,' he added suddenly. 'We're not dealing with a mute child, by any chance? I'm not at all certain that Marchal would have told us; he's a very strange chap, after all!'

'I agree, he is!' Julia said deeply; in fact he was beginning to take on an enormous importance in her mind, a dark importance that she seemed unable to shake off. It even drowned some of her misery about Graham, making her shrug his tentative advances away with an almost absent-minded ease when he was on the ward. She seemed to spend every spare minute puzzling about the child or her uncle.

'I'm sure he would have said something, though. He seems to think that I'm some sort of superhuman nurse. I don't imagine he would keep important information from me.'

'No,' her father agreed, adding with a sudden laugh. 'He has mentioned you to me. He was not entirely specific, but I gained the impression that I was to allow myself to be guided by your judgement as far as Justine was concerned.'

'Oh, really!' Julia said irritably. 'He's the most impossible man! I'll speak to him about Justine, though. He'll be here soon.'

'Tell me tonight, then, darling,' Paul Redford said. He glanced at the small French girl through the window in the office, grinning and waving, and Julia felt her heart quicken as Justine smiled slowly and carefully waved back.

'Well!' Julia's father looked across at her and their eyes met in mutual understanding. 'Find out something from that odd Frenchman, Julia,' he said quietly. 'Don't be fobbed off! There's something quite wrong here and we'd better know what it is as soon as possible!'

She tackled Luc Marchal as soon as he arrived, taking him into the office and closing the door firmly.

'I don't suppose that Justine speaks English, *monsieur*,' she asked seriously.

'As a matter of fact, she does,' he informed her, his dark eyes intent on her.

'Then she does actually speak?' Julia asked carefully, grimacing at his raised eyebrows and startled expression. 'What I'm getting at,' she said determinedly, deciding to come straight out with it, 'is to ask you whether or not there is something about Justine that we should have been told. Is she perfectly normal, Monsieur Marchal?'

'She was!' he said coldly, his eyes narrowing suspiciously. 'If she is now different, then Professor Redford is not the great surgeon that his reputation suggests! What has happened to her?' He stood, towering over Julia, his face threatening, but she was not easily intimidated, although her heart did give a sudden and alarming thump.

'She has been back down for X-rays, for tests and examinations. Physically, Justine is in excellent condition. I think, however—*we* think that she is either unable or unwilling to speak.'

For a second he stood and looked down at her menacingly, and then he turned to the window and swept the curtain aside, his dark gaze vibrantly on the small child who slept peacefully.

'I know this already!' he said in a frightening voice. 'I was not willing to believe it, I waited for you to tell me. Clearly, you imagine that she was not normal before this accident, that I kept things from you. I did not! She was as I told you at the very first, lively, a little wild— and very talkative!' He spun round, his eyes hard on her face. 'I do not blame you. Once again you are vigilant. If Justine has lost the power of speech it is because of some mistake during the operation! Where is Professor Redford now? I will see him at once!'

'You will do no such thing!' Julia snapped, standing and facing him angrily. 'Is it normal with you, Monsieur Marchal, to place the blame squarely on others? There is no motor damage whatever. Every test is clear and to all intents and purposes Justine is now cured!'

'Something has been missed!' he rasped. 'It is a mistake because your father has not operated for some time.'

'My father does not make mistakes!' Julia flared, all hospital discipline forgotten at this attack on her father, but he showed no sign of backing down.

'He made a tragic mistake once,' he grated, 'and you have both been paying for it since then!'

If he had struck her she could not have felt pain so suddenly or so blindingly. Her face paled to chalk-white, her deep blue eyes looking at him in stunned disbelief.

'Lucy had an incurable brain tumour,' she said in a whisper. 'Nothing could have saved her. He knows that. He knew it then. It was merely desperation that forced him to operate. He took all the blame upon himself for no good reason except that we loved her.'

Tears poured down her face and she made no attempt to stem the flow, the hospital, her duties, this hard man forgotten in her wave of misery.

'Forgive me! *Mon Dieu,* I am a heathen!' He reached across and pulled her into his arms, his hand against her hair, forcing her head to his chest. 'You have fought for a life that is dear to me and all I give in return is pain! Forgive me, Julia. Please!'

'My name is Sister Redford,' she said in a shaken voice, straightening up and pulling away from the rather frightening feeling of comfort that was growing very rapidly.

'For a moment it was not,' he said quietly. He reached out and adjusted her white frilled cap, his eyes shocked at his own savagery. 'Now that you are back to normal, though, I can ask you a question. What are we going to do about Justine, Sister Redford?'

'We are going to get to the bottom of it!' Julia said determinedly, wiping her eyes. 'We are going to do it methodically and clinically, and we are not going to rage at anyone for that time!'

'We will try not to,' he agreed and, for the first time ever, Julia saw a smile in his eyes. It went some way to banish her sudden grief, but it did not fool her for one

minute. Here was a hard man, a savage man, a man who
was clearly quite accustomed to issuing orders and having
them obeyed. He would take a lot of careful handling
and she was not at all sure if she could manage it. Time
alone would tell. She indicated that he should go in to
see Justine who was now stirring, and as he went to the
bed she watched them through the window. The child's
hand came out to him at once, a smile on her lips as she
lifted her face for a kiss. They were a strange pair, secret
and dark.

Julia drew the curtain across and left the office, going
back on to the shining brightness of the ward. Luc and
Justine Marchal did not fit in here in any way. They
were alien, locked in a world that would be hard to enter.
Somehow, though, she would have to gain entrance or
Justine would never speak again. Some deep inner con-
viction told her that, and she was prepared to back her
instincts. Graham was on the ward and she passed him
almost without noticing. Another man was on her mind,
she realised, a dark and forbidding man with a very difficult problem. She had not the slightest doubt that Luc
Marchal would expect her to solve it for him.

Again he was waiting for her as she left the hospital,
but this time she had expected it. She got into his car
without any hesitation, knowing quite well that if she
was to get close enough to Justine to help then she would
first have to get close to her uncle.

'It must be clear to you that we should speak to each
other privately,' he said quietly as he drove her home.
'In the hospital you are too busy. I am asking you again
to have dinner with me.'

'Very well,' Julia said evenly, secretly amused at his surprise. It was a small victory to be able to surprise Monsieur Marchal.

'Tonight?' he asked with great care.

'Yes, *monsieur*. I shall be ready at seven-thirty if you would like to pick me up then.'

'And the Professor?' he asked eagerly. 'We could have a joint discussion.'

'No!' Julia said firmly. 'My father has been operating for most of the afternoon. He will be very tired.'

'And you have been working all the day but you are not tired?' he enquired softly. 'What you really mean, Sister Redford, is that you will not allow the opportunity for me to get close enough to your father to question him. Still, I agree! You are protective of Justine, I cannot expect that you are not like that with others, especially your own father. It is your character. I will be honoured to take you to dine.'

'For a discussion about Justine only, *monsieur*!' Julia reminded him firmly. 'If I am to discover nothing helpful then the time will have been wasted.'

'I will not count it wasted, *mademoiselle*!' he said mockingly. 'I have said that it will be an honour and I meant it.'

She wasn't quite sure how to take that and there was only one way to deal with him in any case—a businesslike way. She nodded pleasantly as he dropped her at her house and walked straight in, glad to shut the door behind her and cut him off from her life for a while.

Her father got a very severely edited version of the meeting with the Frenchman at the hospital and then she told him about her dinner-date.

'Straight in at the deep end as usual, darling?' he asked quietly, watching her face.

She knew what he meant. She had always thrown herself resolutely into her work. It was this total commitment to life that had led her to be so involved with Graham. She had been hurt badly and Paul Redford knew it.

'Just take care that you don't get in out of your depth,' he said softly. 'This Frenchman is a handsome devil, and the most determined man I've ever seen.'

'Daddy, he's a lunatic!' Julia said in a scandalised voice.

'That's all right, then!' he laughed. 'Speak to him calmly and carefully.' She had already tried that! She seemed to get on better when she raged at him, although she suspected that she had merely seen the very tip of his rage. There would certainly be a lot more floating underneath.

CHAPTER THREE

HE NEEDED no suggestion as to where they should dine.
He simply took her to the best place, and she was pleased
in spite of everything to see that many people who knew
both herself and Graham were there. It was some small
consolation that they saw her with a very handsome man
and would assume that she was not pining for any lost
love. There was a firm protective air about Luc Marchal
that was very obvious, and Julia knew that people would
draw their own conclusions, even though she knew perfectly well that he was guarding Justine's nurse. If she
should slip and injure herself, he would probably take
the restaurant apart!

She was glad that she had dressed up well. Since her
break-up from Graham she had been in danger of letting
herself go. It had been jeans around the house and then
straight into uniform. She had almost forgotten the
pleasure of being feminine.

She had plenty of clothes, and tonight she wore a
cream silk dress with leaf prints across the skirt, the belt
an exact match for the feathery leaves. She had left her
hair loose, the straight heavy fall of gold shining in the
lights, and Luc's eyes moved over her with unexpected
appreciation.

'It is a pleasure to be your escort, *mademoiselle*,' he
said with a smile that she suspected was sheer mockery.
His tone brought a blush to her smooth cheeks and she

43

was glad that he was behind her, helping her to her seat. Far too many eyes were on them, and she certainly didn't want to make a spectacle of herself.

He sat opposite and instantly the waiter was hovering; Luc Marchal was that sort of a man. She glanced at him from beneath her thick lashes, uneasy at the way he was beginning to fascinate her. Tonight he was relaxed, none of the taut power about him. It might have been an ordinary date and not a meeting to discuss his niece and her wellbeing.

He was very handsome, she admitted, her father was right there. In a dark grey suit, his white shirt startling against his tanned face, his pale grey silk tie perfectly arranged, he looked less alarming, less austere. Away from the hospital and the constant reminder of his problems he seemed to have thawed a little.

She looked away hastily before he could catch her staring at him and as her eyes rose, she gasped in dismay. Across the room sat Graham and his Gloria, her father and mother dining with them, and all their eyes were on her and the handsome Frenchman.

'Ah! You have seen him! I regret, *mademoiselle*, that this has happened, naturally I had no idea that he would be here tonight. If you wish, I will cancel our dinner and we will leave, there are other places to dine.'

'No! It doesn't matter at all!' Realising that she was being sharp, seeming anxious, Julia smiled across at him. 'There's really no reason why...'

'I would not wish to embarrass you. You were engaged to him and now he is about to marry this other girl.'

Her eyes darkened in anger.

'I already know that you have been investigating me, *monsieur*. You told me so before!' she said furiously, her voice low. 'I assume it was to see if I am suitable to care for your niece.'

'You are upset, so I will forgive you that remark,' he said with a warning look at her. 'There is talk in the hospital, as you must know. You are very popular and Doctor Adams is not. The fact that your father is again operating has lifted the spirits of everyone, it seems. It is always a surprise to me that people imagine others to be deaf. I have not investigated you, *mademoiselle*, I have simply listened to other people's conversations!'

'I'm surprised that you listen to gossip, Monsieur Marchal!' Julia said rather desperately, terribly aware of the looks that were coming their way.

'I am interested in you, *mademoiselle*. At the mention of your name I simply—what is your English saying—pricked up my ears?' he said quietly, his hand covering hers on the table, closing tightly around it when she would have moved hers away. 'Leave it!' he ordered. 'Let us give them something to think about, eh?'

When she looked up he was smiling in a mocking, dangerous way, and in spite of everything, she suddenly felt like laughing. Since the advent of Luc Marchal and Justine into her life, she had found that the thought of Graham and his treachery had begun to recede into the very back of her mind. He was utterly worthless and she knew it; only sentimentality had kept her thinking of him at all. Gloria had really done her a favour. She felt her heart lift like magic.

It was surprisingly easy to concentrate on Luc and shut out the others. He was a very dominant man, someone to lean on. The firm hand lingered on hers and then withdrew.

'Good girl!' he murmured, his eyes amused at the way she had pulled herself out of an angry and embarrassed mood. 'Let us talk about Justine. What do you know about us?'

'Oddly enough, nothing,' Julia admitted sarcastically, looking across into his dark, lean face. 'I don't listen to gossip!'

'Touché, mademoiselle!' he applauded with an amused quirk to his lips. 'Then again of course, you are not interested in me, while I am most assuredly interested in you.'

He couldn't be anything but French, Julia thought. The mobile but firm lips, the slant of his eyes, the darkly tinted skin and the underlying, amused assurance he had about him at this moment all spoke of his race. There was something else too, something rather mysterious, but it was impossible to put her finger on that.

'Odd is perhaps an astute choice of word,' he continued drily. 'We are perhaps, to someone like you, an odd family. There is my stepmother, Lucille, my half-sister, Maryse and her brother Philippe,' he paused. 'There was also my brother Jules and his wife Deirdre, Justine's parents, but they were killed in the car accident that I told you of.'

He frowned for a moment and she almost held her breath. He was, in reality, a very forbidding man, and now the unsmiling look that had marked him from the first was back again.

'In this strangely assorted household, it was always difficult for Justine to be herself, to grow, to expand and develop her brightest assets. From the first she was spoiled by everyone except her mother who scolded too much. Since the accident there has been too much gloom surrounding a small child. Lucille is too gentle to be objective, although she tries.'

'After the accident, when you thought that Justine was quite all right, did you notice any difficulty with speech?' Julia interrupted a trifle uneasily.

She had the feeling that he had forgotten the reason for this meeting. His mind seemed to be far into the past, his eyes on her quite unseeing. She had to keep him in the present if any good was to come of this, and she did not like the idea of being drawn into his private affairs in any case. She had the decided feeling that they would be painful!

'No. She was very subdued, especially with me. I was not surprised. I look very much like Jules and I imagine that I was a constant reminder. She spoke well enough though, quite normally. Her chatter was missing, but then that would be normal for a child who had just lost both parents, don't you think?'

He suddenly seemed to be looking into the past again and sighed deeply.

'I have little time to spend on protecting Justine from the worst kinds of adult gloom.' He suddenly laughed softly, his dark eyes narrowing. 'You are thinking no doubt that the reason for the gloom is the fact that I head the household.'

'I was not thinking any such thing!' She flushed, but his amusement was over in any case.

'You imagine, I suspect, that Justine will not speak again ever,' he said bitterly. 'Do you advise that we get other specialists to see her, to make further tests?'

'No! Let's wait a while. I want to try first,' Julia said eagerly, realising that this was completely unprofessional. 'She's still too ill to be moved, in any case,' she added hastily as his eyes focused intently on her flushed face.

She didn't at all like the speculating look in his eyes and sought rapidly to change the direction of the conversation.

'Where exactly do you live, *monsieur*?' she asked, more to bring him away from this intent scrutiny of her face than from any real desire to know. At the mention of his family he had taken on a look of deep brooding. Now he was all attention to her and it filled her with unease.

'We are of the Camargue, *mademoiselle*,' he said quietly and proudly.

'Oh! That's in the south of France, isn't it?'

'*Oui!*' he said looking at her with unsettling vibrancy. 'It is a strange place, a solitary place, a land of sky and water. The Camarguais are not like other people. They do not wish to be!'

'I can quite believe that, Monsieur Marchal,' Julia said wryly.

He suddenly laughed, genuine amusement lighting up his darkly handsome face, turning him into another person, a dangerously attractive person.

'Why do you not call me Luc?' he enquired. 'We are dining out together and it is, after all, my name.'

'I have not been invited to call you by your first name,' Julia reminded him. 'I wouldn't wish to presume.'

'Presume?' he laughed softly. 'I think, *mademoiselle*, that you are a match for me any day, with your softly feminine fears and your bursts of starchy energy. I never quite know whom I am confronting!'

'I never have any doubts on that score with you, *monsieur*!' Julia got out smartly.

'I am alarming?' he enquired softly.

'Quite alien!' she countered, glad even so that the waiter came at that moment.

'It is merely because you do not know me,' he assured her quietly. 'All that will change. Let us eat,' he finished coolly. 'It is better to discuss important things after a meal.'

The feeling of being out-manoeuvred, trapped, came surging over her and she didn't quite know why. She had never met a man like this before, and like an animal she scented danger, though from what direction she did not know. Luc Marchal applied himself to his meal and ignored her.

As she came later from the powder-room Graham was hovering near the bar and walked quickly over to her, stopping her progress back to her own table.

'Doing rather well for yourself, I see!' he snapped angrily. 'Does he know that he's second choice?'

'Does Gloria?' Julia countered with equal anger.

'She doesn't much care so long as she gets what she wants,' he said irritably.

'Do you, so long as it's wealth?' Julia bit out, her dark blue eyes blazing at him.

'You little bitch!' he said in a quiet whisper.

'Only recently! Now, if you'll excuse me, I have a partner of my own.'

'I can see that! Rolling in money and hard as nails,' Graham rasped.

'Oh! You've had a private investigator following him? What a pity I didn't think of that when we were engaged,' Julia said in a sweetly regretful voice. 'Think what I would have discovered!'

'As a matter of fact,' he said morosely, his eyes on her beautiful face, 'Gloria's father recognised him. Monsieur Marchal breeds bulls and horses. Gloria's father breeds horses. It takes one to know one! Marchal is a power in France.'

'He'd be a power anywhere, I imagine,' Julia said quietly, glancing at Luc and then looking rapidly away. There was a dangerous air of annoyance about the handsome face and a shiver ran down her spine.

'He'll go,' Graham said softly, his hand coming to her arm, his fingers beginning to stroke her as they had done so much before, and a feeling of wild irritation filled her, along with an astonished and happy feeling that came from nowhere. She just didn't care! It was like being touched by a stranger! Her life had taken a new turn, a different direction. Nothing that Graham did bothered her at all!

'I still want you, Julia,' Graham said tightly. 'When this is all over, we'll get back together.'

'Not while Gloria is watching as closely as she's watching now!' she said pertly, smiling up at him. 'If you don't take your hand away, I think Luc will be over here, and as you said, he's hard!'

Graham's hand moved away fast and Julia walked back to her table, smiling at Luc as he stood and helped her to her seat.

'He is never going to leave you alone!' he said harshly, his face angry. 'Clearly he desires two women!' He was almost glaring at her and her face flushed wildly at his next comments. 'He has pursued wealth but he cannot give up your beauty. I shall speak to him. I will not have you harassed!'

It was a very violent temper that raged behind his eyes, and Julia stared at him for a second, feeling quite bewildered.

'Shall we go now, Monsieur Marchal?' she asked quietly, her soft question quite startling him when clearly he had expected annoyance.

'Ah! You are treating me like an imbecile again! Obviously I have annoyed you.'

'You could say that,' Julia observed without looking at him, picking up her bag and standing. 'I will help Justine, but I will not be ordered about. The wing you threatened to put over me will be severely burned if you cannot control this urge to dominate! Let me remind you that I do not know you, do not particularly wish to know you and am interested only in Justine's welfare!'

His lips twitched and then he smiled, white teeth against his dark face.

'Your position is stated in no uncertain terms, *mademoiselle*,' he assured her. 'We need you, and I will try to curb my desire to rule the world. We will go as you suggest, any other suggestions and I will gladly obey.'

'Leave Justine to me for a while,' she said determinedly. 'If I can't do anything with her, then when she leaves the hospital my father will find her a specialist who deals with such things.'

'*D'accord!*' he said with a bow. 'Let us depart, *mademoiselle*, while you have the upper hand!'

On Graham's table two people at least were very interested in this intense conversation, and Julia hoped that they did not know that this was a meeting that had ended with sharp words.

Luc's smile grew as he looked at her, almost reading her mind, and his hand reached for hers, holding it firmly and warmly.

'Let us leave in style!' he suggested. 'They will not have the slightest idea where we are going so early in the evening. If I cannot speak severely to your doctor, at least let us leave him with a flourish.'

Julia looked at him wryly, her lips pursed.

'Does the expression bossy-boots mean anything to you?' she enquired mockingly.

'Not entirely,' he confessed with a grin, 'but I can follow the general meaning. You will grow accustomed to it, and after a while, we will not fight.'

'Ah! You'll give in?' she asked flippantly.

'But no, *mademoiselle*,' he assured her. 'I shall expect that of you!'

Julia had a curious light-hearted feeling. It was a long time since she had felt like that. Suddenly, everything was going well. Her father was doing what he had been born to do and his confidence was back. There had been no chance to save Lucy, and deep down inside he knew that, had always known it. The mourning had stayed, even so, but now, with Justine growing stronger every day, he seemed to have come to terms with life all over again. His happiness permeated the house and Julia felt the reflected warmth although they were both busy from morning until night.

There was only the problem of Justine and her refusal to speak. Julia was quite sure it was that. The little girl was now back in her own room almost ready to be discharged. With Julia she was bright and cheerful but no word ever crossed her lips, not one sound.

It seemed that her progress was the only subject of conversation at home but they were getting nowhere. There was not enough time to spend with her and soon Julia would be leaving, her departure almost coinciding with Justine's. It never seemed to have sunk in with Luc Marchal that Justine must soon leave the hospital. He made quick necessary visits to France but was never away for long, reappearing and demanding discussions with Julia, expecting that she would be available to stop everything for him.

She knew that she was being drawn too deeply into their lives, that her attachment to Justine and the child's attachment to her was not good, but she also knew that behind those bright, dark eyes, Justine thought clearly and determinedly kept silent. It was utterly frustrating.

Both Julia and the professor had brushed up their French, talking to Justine and to each other in her presence in her own language. She had still said nothing, although she had smiled at their mistakes. The time was fast running out. Justine would soon be in France and someone else's problem. Julia knew that she would miss her, that she had disobeyed the first rule of nursing and become emotionally attached to a patient, but it had happened almost without her noticing.

She was beginning to be impatient to get on duty every day. In the evenings her mind was taken up with thoughts of the child and her uncle. Justine had steadily taken a place for herself in Julia's heart, a place that had been empty for three years, and she dreaded the day when her resignation would take effect and she would no longer be able to see the child again.

'Here you are, Curly Top!' The sight of Justine sitting up in bed, her head just covered with a fine growth of dark hair, never failed to bring a smile to Julia's lips, although this time she almost lost her poise. She had not seen Luc Marchal arrive, otherwise she would have delayed her visit. What a stupid thought! Her lips tightened at the idea and Justine's face fell.

'You are angry with us, Sister Redford?' Luc Marchal asked in an amused voice, glancing from his niece's face to Julia. 'I cannot think how we have offended. We are sitting here most quietly.'

'I'm not angry,' Julia said with a reassuring smile at Justine, walking briskly forward to the bed and the charts at the end of it, her face slightly flushed. Justine's sharp, dark eyes saw far too much and today Julia felt quite frustrated.

'Oh, you're doing this deliberately, Curly Top, aren't you?' she said quietly to Justine. 'You simply refuse to speak. I would have thought that by now you would want to talk to me.'

The effect of her small burst of frustration was astonishing. Justine looked at her intently, her eyes switching to Luc's face and then back again, and for a second, Julia imagined that she saw fear. But how could it be? Justine waited with impatience for her uncle, threw her arms around him, did everything but speak.

Her eyes came to Luc Marchal's face and he looked steadily back, reading her mind.

'You are quite wrong,' he said quietly.

She was saved from any comment by the staff nurse who came in with an unusual rush.

'We've just found out who your replacement is! Guess who...oh, sorry!' She stopped in confusion at the sight of Julia's face and at the suddenly tight expression on the face of the Frenchman. 'I'll tell you later.' She backed out rapidly but the damage had been done. Julia could see Justine's small forehead creased as she struggled with the meaning of replacement. Luc Marchal was not struggling at all. He was furious!

Julia went along to the office but almost immediately he was there.

'You are leaving, Sister Redford. You are deserting Justine!' he accused her in a dangerously quiet voice.

'My resignation was already handed in long before I even saw your niece, Monsieur Marchal!' Julia replied, angry that he was making her feel guilty when she had nothing whatever to feel guilty about. 'I am not deserting anyone. Justine will be going soon in any case. She's ready to be discharged.'

'Tell me which hospital you are going to and I will have her moved to be with you,' he said decisively, ignoring her comments.

'I'm not going to any hospital yet, *monsieur*.' Julia sat down and then changed her mind. She didn't at all fancy the idea of him towering over her so insistently. 'For a short time I shall not apply to any hospital. I have—have things to sort out.' Like my life, she thought ruefully.

'Then nurse Justine for me!' he said forcefully, even taking her hand. 'I will place her in a private nursing home and you can be with her. I will not take her so far from Professor Redford yet, and I will certainly not take her from you!'

Julia looked at him seriously, a little afraid now of the plan that she and her father had discussed.

'I'm sure I can help her,' she said quietly. 'My father and I have talked about it, and if you feel so strongly that you want her to be close to both of us, then we suggest that when she leaves the hospital, she comes to stay with us for a while. I'll be able to give her my full attention, and if it doesn't work, then both of us feel that at least no harm will have been done.'

Luc was astonished. For a few minutes he just looked at her until she began to feel she had suggested something altogether inappropriate.

'You would do this, for Justine?' he enquired with a very intent look on his face. 'You would take her into your own home?'

'Gladly!' She suddenly found herself smiling. 'Maybe you'll live to regret it. It might be that when the time comes, we'll refuse to let her go.'

'Ah, no!' he said with one of his faint smiles. 'It is the other way around. Justine and I are hanging on very tightly to you! It is you who will be released with reluctance.'

'I do hope you realise it will be for a short time only,' Julia said with a quick flare of unexpected anxiety. 'After all, I have a career, and sooner or later I must get back into a hospital.'

'Oh, I understand,' he said easily, a deep glow beginning in his dark eyes. 'Just for a while. When Justine is stronger, even if she is not speaking, we will say goodbye to you and offer our thanks. Meanwhile, you may just perform a miracle. I know you are capable of that!'

It did nothing to quiet Julia's sudden misgivings. What exactly did he expect of her? How much more would he expect? She had been drawn into his life and now, quite suddenly, she was being drawn in further by her affection for a small child who was nothing to her at all, and by her inability to let go of a problem until it was solved. There was something much more too and it quite frightened her. She wanted no further involvements.

Her father was delighted when she told him that night.

'We'll see what we can do here,' he said vigorously. 'You'll be with her all day and I'll help when I can. At least we'll improve our French!'

Julia looked at him steadily, a little worried now by their decision.

'Are we wise, Daddy?' she asked quietly. 'Are we perhaps letting this get out of hand for—for personal reasons?'

'Perhaps,' he said softly, taking her slim shoulders in his hands and looking down at her anxious face. 'I only know that we're beginning to recover, both of us. If we can help Justine too, then what is the harm?'

'I suppose you're right,' Julia sighed. 'You've got a lot more wisdom than I have.'

'Not according to Luc Marchal,' her father laughed. 'He imagines you are some quite superior being.'

'He's the very limit!' Julia said, turning fretfully away. Goodness knew how she was going to live up to the standards Luc Marchal seemed to have set for her.

'I've been thinking that it would perhaps be a kindness to invite him to stay here too when he's in England,' her father said with a suspiciously nonchalant air. 'It seems a bit mean, Justine here and her uncle staying in an hotel when we've got all this room.'

'No!' Julia turned rapidly to face her father and looked at him in near horror. 'No! No! No! I could not face Luc Marchal day in day out! A small dose at a time is more than enough.'

'Are you scared of getting involved again, Julia?' her father asked quietly. 'You're very beautiful and very loving. Don't let that young puppy Adams ruin your life for ever.'

Graham might very well be a young puppy, but Luc Marchal was far more alarming and lingered in her mind almost constantly, usually worrying her.

'There's no chance of getting involved with him!' she said a trifle sharply, her cheeks somewhat flushed. 'He's like a machine with an inclination to dominate all humanity. His mind is totally on Justine and my supposedly supreme skills. He's irritating and quite impossible!'

'Well, that's boxed him up nicely,' her father laughed. 'Maybe you should help him to improve by telling him all that?'

'I have!' Julia said impatiently. 'I've told him in a variety of different ways. He can't seem to take it in!

Justine would improve more if he were constantly in France.'

'I don't think so, darling,' Paul Redford said quietly. 'That child loves him dearly.'

'I know,' Julia murmured, almost to herself. 'Isn't it strange, though, that she looks so anxious each time they meet? She needs to hear him speak for a while before the anxiety dies down. I wonder what she's dreading.'

CHAPTER FOUR

IT WAS almost a month before Luc decided that Justine should return to the Camargue. For Julia and her father it had been a month of pure joy mixed with frustration. The little girl had simply slipped into their lives with ease and the yawning gap that had held them all in unhappiness had closed and healed. She had not, however, spoken one single word and they had all given up, even Julia. It was time to hand Justine over to someone trained in the field, but Julia was still convinced that the reason lay not too deeply below the surface.

She had tried everything. Her French was now very good, because she had decided that for a child so young it would be better to coax her in her own language. Even Mrs Dobson tried the odd word, but nothing worked. Free now from the hospital, Julia took to her old hobby of painting, her watercolours constantly out, Justine fascinated by the birds and flowers that grew from the swift strokes of her brush, but although the child pointed and became sometimes very excited, she said nothing.

'Julia has greatly improved her French, *ma belle*!' Luc said one day when he visited. 'She is doing very well. It would be even better if you could help her, I think.'

The trick did not succeed, but Justine ran into another room and came back with some of the paintings, embarrassing Julia and bringing her father into instant action as he joined in to show off her work. He was not long going into his study and bringing back more of her efforts either, and Luc looked at her with a different respect.

'You are very talented,' he assured her, his eyes on the fresh and glowing colours of the flowers and birds that her father had always had framed. 'Why did you decide to be a nurse instead?'

'I'm not good enough to earn my living as an artist. I do it now to help me to relax,' Julia said quietly, giving her father a look of exasperation. She did not particularly want to have those dark eyes drawn to her. Luc Marchal was a very disturbing man and often, when he came to see Justine, he spent a great deal of time with his unfathomable gaze on Julia's face. She wished to avoid it, not draw it to her. He made her feel too excited inside in a queer and troubled way. She was quite unused to feelings like this and she did not welcome them.

Luc had spent more time in France once he was satisfied that Justine was settled and Julia was becoming increasingly nervous every time he called. The next time he came however there was a different air about him and it was with a terrible shock that Julia faced the reality of the end of all this. He came one weekend and announced that the next week would be Justine's last in England.

'You have found yourself a new family, *ma belle*!' he said as Justine curled in his lap. 'It is an addition, though, not to replace your own family. Next week, you will return to your own land and say goodbye to your friend Julia.'

His eyes noted the sudden sadness in Julia's face, but not one of them was prepared for the reaction of Justine to this news. She stiffened in surprise, her eyes on Luc and then on Julia, and before anyone could react or soothe her she was out of Luc's arms, racing across to where Julia sat, her arms outstretched to be flung wildly around Julia's neck as she launched herself upon her.

'*Non!*' It was a small voice, almost rusty with lack of use. '*Non!* Come, Julia! Come! *Venez avec moi!*'

Sheer delight grew on Julia's face, tears springing to her eyes as she met Luc Marchal's dark and startled gaze.

'*Ciel!*' he breathed. '*C'est incroyable!*'

They were all on their feet, Paul Redford grinning widely, Julia laughing and crying as she hugged the weeping child who clung to her and refused to let go, and Luc who seemed to be stunned into immobility, his night-black eyes vividly on Julia's glowing face.

For a while there was turmoil and then Julia calmed Justine and suggested that she be put to bed for a small sleep. The effort and the emotion had exhausted the little girl and she clung to Julia's neck, her sobbing now soft and quiet as she was carried away.

Paul Redford took Luc upstairs after a few minutes and silently pointed to the half-opened door of Justine's room. Julia sat on the bed, the little girl's hands in her own and softly, carefully she coaxed words from the once silent lips.

'Have a quick look at her, Daddy, will you?' Julia said as she came quietly out to them later. 'She seems to be all right, but it was as big a shock to her as it was to us. Her pupils are a little dilated. I'd be happier if you'd just check.' She turned to Luc with a rather shaky smile as her father went in to Justine. 'I think we need a cup of tea, *monsieur*!' she said tremulously. 'Let's go down to the kitchen.'

Mrs Dobson had gone and Julia walked into the bright kitchen to make a drink, her hands still shaking. She was not aware how close Luc stood until he suddenly swung her around with an almost impatient air about him.

'Julia!' he said vibrantly, just standing perfectly still, his dark eyes burning into hers. 'Julia!' He suddenly drew her into his arms, holding her tightly, his face in her hair.

'Come, Julia! Come!' he begged harshly. 'Come with us to France.' He lifted his head and looked into her startled eyes. *'Venez avec moi!'* he said desperately, exactly like Justine. And Julia knew right then that she would go. The door to the heart of this strange and aloof man was wide open just this once, and she wanted to walk inside more than she had wanted anything in her whole life.

Even so, as they flew out to France the next week she wondered if she had done the right thing. That Justine was delighted there was no doubt and, after the dramatic recovery of the child's speech, Paul Redford had agreed that to separate her from Julia at this stage would be unwise. He agreed with Luc also that it was time that Justine returned to her own home, and although he did not mention it, he clearly considered that it would be better for Julia to be with Justine when the little girl faced again the situation that they both felt had brought all this on in the first place.

At Luc's insistence, her watercolours were packed in her luggage. There was little to do to pass the time for someone who had lived in or near a city for most of her life, he had told her. When Justine was with her tutor, Julia would be able to make a permanent record of her stay in the Camargue. It took her fancy and she was glad she had brought them. It was something to hang on to because she had not the slightest doubt that she was about to enter a very alien atmosphere, and the calm of the Women's Surgical ward suddenly seemed to be very far away.

She had never asked about Luc's home or even about the Camargue itself, and she was stunned into silence when they arrived. They had driven from Marseilles and though the distance was not great, the change to another world was almost frightening.

Luc had called it a land of sky and water, a different land, and it was that. Bounded by the sea to the south, by the two arms of the Rhône, the area was a vast water-jewelled plain of great variety. There was a huge area of wilderness that sheltered migratory birds, there were rice fields and shimmering salt flats and great areas of grassland where the fierce bulls of the Camargue were reared on *manades*, ranches. That was where Luc lived, and that was their destination.

He drove close to the Etang de Vaccarès and stopped the car as Julia gasped in amazement to see great flights of flamingoes rise above the water, their beauty turning the sky pink as they wheeled and turned to seek other feeding grounds.

'You are glad now that you brought your paints?' he with quiet amusement, his eyes on her entranced face.

'Oh! If only I had the skill!' she whispered, her wide eyes following their flight.

'I think that you have,' he insisted. 'I will see to it that you get the opportunity.'

'I'm here to help Justine, don't forget,' Julia reminded him, turning reluctantly away and finding his eyes on her face.

'Not all the time,' he assured her, watching her steadily. 'You will not find Justine too difficult, and I will see to it that nobody else presents any difficulty for you.'

For a second she looked back at him, and they sat in a silence that was almost breathtaking. She had no idea how she looked. In a blue linen suit that was almost the colour of her eyes, her thick, fair hair caught up into a loose knot, strands of gold escaping to curve around her delicate face, she might have been as much a child as Justine but for the ripe perfection of her breasts, the slender elegance of her legs.

Luc's eyes roamed over her slowly, and only then did she realise that she too was openly regarding him, seeing anew the lean, dark, handsome face, the thick black hair now tossed by the wind that blew across the Camargue. Their eyes met and held and there was no smile in his gaze, merely a questioning and probing vibrancy that brought her breath out in a long, shuddering sigh. Something was happening between them and she had no idea what it was. A great flare of awareness raced through her and she tore her gaze away, her cheeks flushing wildly.

'*Oncle* Luc can see that nobody is difficult!' Justine asserted after a puzzled glance at both of them. '*Oncle* Luc is very important, he is the Marquis de Saint-Michaud! And that is *very* important!'

'Be quiet, *s'il te plaît*, Justine!' he said sharply, his lips twisting wryly as her face fell.

'But it is true! Why should not Julia know, *Oncle* Luc? Everyone else knows and Julia is our friend, *n'est-ce pas*?' she finished with a frown, and then subsided into silence, curling up on the back seat of the car and closing her eyes as if to shut out everything.

Now that they were back, the chatter that had grown over the past week was beginning to slow down and Julia felt that she must be alert, watchful. She did not want to start all over again with a silent child. Luc's quick reproof had gone very deep with Justine.

'It really doesn't matter, Justine,' Julia said hastily, her eyes reproachful on Luc's dark face. 'I really don't mind who Uncle Luc is. Nobody is important to me, except you!'

'That is nice!' Justine sprang up and threw her arms around Julia's neck. 'Now I shall not share you with *Oncle* Luc until he has stopped being cross with me!'

'I have stopped! I regret my annoyance, *petite*!' he said with a mockingly anxious look at her that had Julia laughing.

'Then we are all friends again!' Justine drew him into the stranglehold of her embrace. 'I have a great fancy to see *Grand-maman* Lucille! Can we go now?'

'But of course!' Luc swung the car away from the water and turned to the road and Julia was silent. Justine was going to be a constant problem. She was talking again, but they had no idea why she had stopped in the first place. It was perhaps the accident, the loss of her parents. She had never once mentioned them, the desire to see her grandmother the only mention she had ever made of home. It was disturbing. It was not, however, as disturbing as the discovery of Luc's title, and the feelings that had seemed to arc between them when their eyes had met.

Here, in the Camargue, a cloak seemed to have fallen from him and he was subtly different. Uneasiness flooded through Julia and she stared at the straight road, telling herself that she was merely doing a favour, that she could go home whenever the mood took her. Why was it, then, that one surreptitious glance at the dark and capable hands on the wheel made her doubt that?

He had called her Justine's friend; who would be a friend to her in this new and strange land? With every mile, Luc had changed, and she knew without any doubt that she was now in his territory, with his people.

She took a deep breath and straightened her back, her mouth firm and resolute, almost jumping to find Luc's dark eyes glancing across at her, a quick and brilliant glance like summer lightning.

'You have decided to delay your escape until some future date, Julia?' he queried drily. 'You have courage, *ma chère*, but it will not be needed against me. We are in this together, for Justine's sake. Try to remember that when you find me so—alien!'

The Manade de Michaud was a surprise to Julia. What she had been expecting, she did not quite know. Perhaps some ranch in the manner of the American West. This was utterly different. Night was rapidly approaching and the gathering dusk made everything seem more unreal.

They entered high white gates and drove along a private road that led to the house and Julia could feel tension mounting in Justine although the child said nothing. In this quiet and mysterious landscape, Justine began to seem as unreal as Luc, as darkly alien. She must pull herself together and not allow this moodiness to grip her.

On either side, the ferny tamarisk trees cast shadows over the road and the car seemed to sweep from sunlight into shadow with every foot of the journey. Beyond the trees was land, vast stretches of it, that was home to the fierce black bulls raised here; over two hundred on Luc's ranch, Justine had told her, but they were not visible now although she watched for them rather fearfully.

Among the trees though a small herd of white horses grazed, ghostly in the gathering dusk, their heads tossing impatiently at the passing of the car.

'They look almost wild!' Julia said in an awe-stricken voice, and Luc's cool, dark voice was tinged with mockery.

'Mostly, they are! Surely you have heard of the white horses of the Camargue? A few of them are used to work on the ranches but they are not confined, the rest wander at will by the *étangs*, the marshes. From time to time, we have a drive, that is something to see, the *gardians* with their tridents herding the horses to the ranch!'

'Gardians?' Julia asked in a subdued voice, wondering how she could have been so stupid as to imagine that she was merely coming to France. This place seemed as unreal as to be another continent.

'Cowboys, *mademoiselle*!' he informed her mockingly. 'You will find them quite romantic I imagine because I strongly suspect that under that calm exterior there lurks a romantic. You are not always calm.'

And that's a fact! Julia thought with a sudden shiver. It was becoming increasingly difficult to stay calm and face Luc Marchal. This was not the ordered existence of the hospital or her own home, although that had been difficult enough. This was his own home territory, and she suspected that he was something like a king here in his own land.

Unexpectedly they swung around the long narrow road and came to a white fence and sweeping lawns, and the rather wild stretches of tree and grassland gave way to ordered beauty. The gardens were ablaze with summer flowers, trees and bushes filled with colour, the glitter of a pool around the side of the house, and the house itself, a long, white house of considerable size, built in the Provençal manner, gabled, attractive and somehow comforting.

'We have arrived!' Luc said softly. 'Welcome to my home, Julia. From this moment forward, you are my guest as Justine was yours. If there is any way that we can repay your kindness and care we will do it.'

'I have no desire to be repaid, *monsieur*!' Julia said a trifle anxiously, and he turned to her with his faintly mocking smile.

'Luc!' he corrected firmly. 'Please do not call me *monsieur*. As to repayment, I do not have to be able to read your mind to know that we are but at the beginning of the cure for Justine. You act purely from instinct and from compassion but you will fathom it all out, of that I am sure. My debt of gratitude will then be beyond price. I have told you that I am very busy for most of the time. I want Justine to be in your care and I will tell the family that you are to have total control over her. I have complete faith in you.'

'But I'm an outsider, a visitor! What will they...?' she began uneasily.

'Leave them to me,' he said sharply. 'Justine is still very vulnerable, likely to go back to silence as well you know. She needs you, and I will not allow interference!'

So he was back to that! Julia felt very vulnerable herself. One false step and the whole thing would come crashing down. She had the uneasy feeling that she would be the one to feel the blow.

There was nothing further to say. Justine remained in the car with a marked reluctance to step down in spite of her expressed desire to see *Grand-maman* Lucille, and in the end it was Luc who lifted her out, keeping her hand in his as her other hand stole quietly into Julia's as if she were about to face a great ordeal.

Julia looked up at the house in the gathering dusk, hearing the strange sounds around her, the night music of the Camargue. There was no going back now, at least not yet. Luc's proud face told her that, and the little hand that clenched and unclenched in her own told her even more loudly. For better or for worse she was in Luc's land, at the Manade de Michaud, home of Luc Marchal, Marquis de Saint-Michaud. She had agreed to come here, had found within her a great love for Justine. Luc had changed all their lives for the better and she should be happy. Why then did she feel like a captive? It was a question she did not care to answer.

Later, as Julia unpacked her things and changed for dinner in the comfortable and airy room close to Justine's room she asked herself what she had been worrying about. They loved the child, every one of them. She had been completely wrong. Nothing here could have led to Justine's silence.

Her mind went back to their arrival and she realised that she was looking forward to going back downstairs. In their way, they were all strange but there was something about them that was exciting. They were very different from any people she had known. She was intrigued, and felt almost as if she were merely on holiday.

Justine had behaved a little oddly as they came into the house, turning her face into Julia's warmth, her hand releasing Luc. With no hesitation, Julia lifted her. Slender though Julia was herself, the little girl was still light and fragile-looking from her ordeal, and Julia was filled again with the need to protect her.

The house was beautiful, warm and well kept; surely there was nothing here to frighten a child? Julia's eyes met Luc's as his gaze rested narrowed and puzzled on Justine and then on her. He seemed to be about to speak, but anything he would have said was forestalled as a woman came quietly into the room.

'Justine, *ma petite*! You are home at last!' Her arms opened wide and, as Julia allowed Justine to slide to the floor, she flew across to her grandmother.

'*Grand-maman* Lucille! I have wanted to see you! I have missed you!' She was enfolded tightly in two warm arms and the dark eyes that met Julia's were warm too. She was perhaps fifty, Julia thought, but she was not like Luc in any way. She did not have the haughty bearing, the austere face. There was some extra thing about her that defied description, a sharp gleam in the dark eyes, an extra quality to the nut-brown face. Whereas Luc was golden brown, his stepmother was almost swarthy, and her eyes had a knowing look that was at once amusing and uncanny.

'You are Sister Redford?' she asked softly, her hand stroking and soothing on Justine's short and tender hair. 'Luc has told us of your great kindness to Justine, and also of your father's great skill.'

'The *professeur* is the best in the world and lives in a great house. He is very important!' Justine said, looking up at her grandmother. 'He also is my friend and he tosses me in the air. I will go back to England with Julia one day and live with them!'

'Hush, child,' Lucille Marchal said softly. 'Who is more important than you? If you leave us we will shrivel like the grass on the marshes. You are greatly loved.'

'Ah, rascal! You are home!' The voice from the doorway had Justine squealing with pleasure and she launched herself into yet new arms as a young man of Julia's own age stood dramatically poised to receive her.

'Philippe!' She was caught into two arms and held high in the air before he turned to smile at Julia.

'Ah! You have brought us an English princess!' he said, looking at Julia with open admiration. 'I have heard you boasting about her importance. I am pleased that you are back to making much noise, *chérie*. It has been quiet without you.'

'In Julia's house I did not speak!' Justine said quietly, her thin arms around his neck. 'I had to speak though at last, because she was going to stay behind and not come with me. It was necessary to speak then.'

'Perhaps this English princess spoils you,' Philippe said softly, his eyes beginning to roam appreciatively over Julia's figure.

'The English princess is a very strict sister in a hospital!' Luc said a little sharply, coming forward to take Julia's arm. 'I will introduce you properly, now that the initial skirmish is over,' he added drily. 'Lucille, my stepmother, and Philippe, my half-brother.'

He nodded to each in turn, his manner a little cool, his grip on Julia's arm unnecessarily tight.

'Sister Redford, who has very kindly offered to leave her career in abeyance and come here to help Justine. You will call her Julia. She will be one of the family and she is to have a free hand entirely with Justine. She is answerable only to me!'

'And you, as we know, are answerable to no one!' Philippe quipped, his handsome face breaking into smiles when Luc's narrowed eyes were turned on him. 'I do but jest!' he said with amusing haste. 'I have seen what happens to those who cross swords with you, big brother.'

'If you continue to play the fool you may well find one day that it is exactly what you are!' Luc said sardonically. 'For now I will show Julia to her room and I will offer you the privilege of carrying up her luggage. Where is Maryse?' he suddenly asked sharply.

'She is late this evening, but she will be in for dinner!' Lucille said quickly, and Julia was oddly relieved to see Luc's hand come to his stepmother's shoulder, a look of understanding and liking pass between them. It was not all to be battle in this house, then. Clearly he resented his brother's attitude towards her. She hoped that he did not feel that Philippe would become a problem in her way. There would clearly be sparks flying if Luc was to continue this hard attitude.

'Come, *ma belle*!' Luc said to Justine as Philippe lowered her to the floor. 'Use those legs to walk to your room. If you let Julia look around she may decide that the walls are too bare and need perhaps a picture or two. Who knows, she may even paint one for you.'

'You are also an artist, Julia?' Philippe asked admiringly, his handsome face alive with interest.

'A wonderful artist!' Justine boasted.

'And very important!' Luc said drily, turning his charges to the door and urging them out of the room.

He had shown her the room that was to be hers and then he had left, no doubt to go back to making her position here quite clear, she thought a little angrily. She was not about to throw her weight about when Lucille and Philippe so obviously loved Justine. She wondered what Maryse was like. Philippe did not resemble his mother, except perhaps for a certain harshness of skin. He was more like Luc in looks but with an altogether softer, handsome look. Was Maryse like that? Was she any problem?

She finished dressing, impatient with herself for all this detective work. It was quite ridiculous. It became more apparent by the minute that Justine's silence was some sort of trauma after the accident. Perhaps her illness had prevented it from happening before.

Tonight she wanted to look good, to have everything going well. She would not be here for long. For the first time since the operation she felt quite at ease about

Justine and as soon as it became apparent to Luc he would be quite agreeable to her going home.

Her jersey trousers were tight in the leg and the matching loose top with wide sleeves were a deep purple, a startling contrast to her richly golden hair. She had left her hair loose, swept back behind her ears, silver earrings dangling and catching the light. With a silver bangle on her wrist, high-heeled silver sandals on her small and perfect feet, Julia looked almost eastern, very exotic. It was a sophisticated outfit and she was pleased with it.

At the tap on her door she smiled at the thought of Justine and called out merrily, 'Come in, Justine!'

It was Luc, his tall frame resplendent in a dark suit, his icily blue shirt brilliant against his deeply golden skin.

'Justine has been given her supper in bed,' he said quietly, his eyes on her startling beauty. 'She is over-excited and even now falling asleep.'

'Oh! I'll go to her!' She made to move forward but he shook his head, stopping her.

'No. Let her simply drift off to sleep. Tomorrow will be soon enough for you to take responsibility for Justine. For tonight, simply be my guest.'

Her sudden movement had left her standing in the centre of the room and she felt extremely vulnerable, over-conscious of her own body and shamefully conscious of his. He simply watched her, a habit that he seemed to have had since their first meeting, his dark eyes intent on her face.

'You think that it is I, do you not?' he asked quietly.

For a moment she failed to understand and then her cheeks flushed, but she held her ground.

'No, not now. I admit that at first I thought it possible. Justine loves you, but she sometimes gives you very
odd looks.'

'I can only agree.' He walked slowly further into the
room and leaned against the dressing-table, his legs
crossed elegantly, his hands in his pockets. 'She has been
like that since the accident. I assume that it is my like-
ness to Jules, as I have said before. What do you think
now, though, as you appear to have discarded that idea?'

'Probably delayed shock,' Julia said firmly. She didn't
like this conversation and she didn't like him here in her
room. 'We'll give it a week, and if she's still all right,
I'll go home.'

'That is an idea that I have not yet considered,' he
said quietly. 'I think you will find our need for you
stretches far longer than any week.'

'Justine understands that I have my own work to do!'
Julia said as forcefully as possible.

'She understands,' Luc said softly. 'But will she tolerate your departure?'

Julia felt trapped. Every instinct told her to settle this
matter here and now.

'Sooner or later I shall have to go!' she said sharply.
'I've helped as much as I have been able, but there will
obviously be an end to this. Justine will settle here and
I'll be less important to her. It will happen very quickly.
Lots of young patients take a great liking for their nurses,
even grown-ups do it. When they settle at home, they
don't even remember your name. That's how it should
be!' she finished starchily.

'Justine is not just any child, though,' Luc said vibrantly. 'Deirdre was never really a mother to her, she

did not want a child. Justine has never known a mother's love. When Jules was alive, it did not matter so much, he gave her all the love she could wish for. Now, the whole state of affairs is painfully clear to her, and she has a memory.'

'How dreadful!' Julia looked at him in silence, her deep blue eyes shocked.

'Children tend to take matters into their own hands,' he said softly. 'She has relatives who love her, but it is not enough. She loves me, but again that is not enough. As we came into the house I could not help but notice that she left me to go to you. You have puzzled over her and so have I. I have solved my puzzle. Justine has decided that she needs a mother. I think that she has chosen you!'

'That's impossible!' Julia stared at him a little wildly. 'My stay here is very temporary. You know that! If I had suspected any such thing I would never have come. It's best for her to have a clean break from me if that's how she feels! Of course,' she added, 'it's only your opinion!'

'An opinion I have had for some time!' he assured her.

Then she saw the trap that she had walked into. 'Come to France with us, Julia.' *'Venez avec moi!'* Just what did he expect her to do now? He had deliberately manoeuvred her here to the Camargue thinking this! She had done well to fear this dark, strange man.

'I am not always here, Julia,' he continued before she could reply. 'We have business interests in other parts of France. We live here only because we are Camarguais and enjoy the wilderness. Our wealth is in hotels on the

Riviera, in vineyards and in many other things. It is necessary for me to travel, therefore, we need you, Justine and I.'

'As what, exactly, *monsieur*?' Julia asked tightly, her eyes beginning to take on the old aggression.

'As a friend most assuredly,' he remarked with a mocking smile. 'What else could you be?'

'I could not be a substitute mother, for one thing!' Julia snapped. 'I'm very fond of Justine, but I have a life of my own and a country of my own. As I said before, we'll give it a week!'

'We will see,' he said infuriatingly. 'Until then, do not spread your compassion around too freely, English princess! It may be that very soon I would greedily accept it and I am sure that Philippe would accept it from the first, the way he looked at you tonight. Concentrate on Justine and leave everyone else to defend themselves.'

'I'll remember that, *monsieur*!' she said stiffly, her stance back to the sister at St Andrews.

'Luc!' he corrected mildly, his smile growing at her flustered appearance. 'Come, let me escort you to dinner!' She walked slowly forward, a little anxious at the necessity to pass so close to his powerfully masculine body, and his hand shot out unexpectedly, capturing her face and tilting it to the light.

'You are dazzlingly beautiful!' he said steadily. 'And yet, I do not know if you even realise it. In many ways you are a child yourself, but I know that Justine is safe always with you. Come, *ma belle*! Let us face things together!'

He took her arm politely, escorting her from the room, but the feelings that began to race through her as soon as his hand touched her were molten and frightening. He was some dark power who had re-shaped her life and suddenly, like a child, she longed for her father. What had he meant? As far as she was concerned there was nothing at all to face. She would go home as soon as possible. This had been a very foolish idea!

CHAPTER FIVE

THE OTHER member of the family was there when they went downstairs, Maryse, Luc's half-sister. Her relationship to Philippe was obvious and she had her mother's strangely knowing eyes.

Dark, with long black hair that reached her waist, there was a rather haughty beauty about her that was spoiled by her look of antagonism, an expression that seemed to be well established. She greeted Luc with a stare that was both worried and defiant.

'The bank is working late nowadays?' he enquired softly, a certain amount of steel behind the quiet question.

Julia would have liked to wander off to some other part of the charming room but his hand was as firm on her arm as a clamp.

'I am eighteen! I can do as I please!' Maryse tossed her head and raised her chin, meeting his gaze with a blushing anger like a child who had been caught out in some mischief.

'You are lucky! At thirty-six I do not do as I please!' Luc said irascibly. 'I do what is expected of me. You will do the same and cause less worry to your mother!'

'It's all right, Luc,' Lucille said quickly, her face anxious, but Maryse interrupted before Luc could reply.

'There is nobody to tell you what to do, Luc!' she snapped angrily. 'You are the complete master here and we do not *know* what you do!'

Her dark eyes flicked to Julia with the merest suggestion of query and Luc exploded.

'Insolence with me does not pay!' he grated, his face darkening in fury. 'If you also intend to insult my guest then you will be expected to eat in your room for the duration of her stay. I will not have Mademoiselle Redford upset under any circumstances! You will now apologise to her for that sly little look that contained so much venom!'

'I am sorry, Luc.' The dark head fell beneath this onslaught and Julia tightened up inside with embarrassment. 'I am sorry, Mademoiselle Redford. I really do know why you are here and we are all grateful.'

'J'espère bien!' Luc rasped, his face still tight with anger. 'Tomorrow I will see this man at the bank. You are a *jeune fille* and not to be put at risk!'

'Oh, please, Luc!' Maryse looked utterly defeated, but Luc waved his hand dismissively.

'That is enough! This is Julia's first meal with us. Let us try to behave as a family. It is what she is accustomed to and what she expects.'

'And she is an English princess of *great* importance!' Philippe ventured boldly before Luc's flashing dark eyes stopped that line of banter promptly.

With his hand still tight on her arm, Luc led Julia into the next room to dine and she felt as upset as Maryse appeared to be now that her attempt at defiance had been crushed so harshly. It had not mattered to Luc that there was a stranger here tonight. He had wielded discipline ruthlessly and immediately. He was the master and clearly they all knew that. Julia could not help wondering how he behaved under normal circumstances. His sharp query as he had noticed Maryse's absence when they had arrived and his anger now showed that he took full responsibility for everyone here. It rather put into perspective his demands upon her.

During the meal, tempers cooled, even Luc's, and although Maryse was mostly silent except for the odd remark she made to Philippe, her eyes strayed to Julia from time to time and finally she smiled a rather tentative smile which Julia returned wholeheartedly. When Lucille questioned her about her job, about Justine's operation and about her own father, Julia was glad to be able to talk and help to ease the strain that had lingered among them. They were all interested, and Maryse particularly.

'I would be interested in being a nurse,' Maryse said as they went into the salon, her words meant for Julia's ears alone.

'*Ciel!* Next you will want to be a brain surgeon!' Philippe said with a laugh, ducking as she aimed a playful blow at him.

'Julia is only twenty-four and already she is a sister,' Luc reminded Maryse with a rather indulgent look that took Julia by surprise after his sharp words to the girl earlier. 'Can you even imagine the hard work that that has entailed? You are very much like a butterfly, *petite*. I think that the idea of beginning at the bottom and working your way up would be too much for you. You cannot start as a sister. Julia has great skills.'

This extravagant praise startled and embarrassed Julia. She had no desire to be the focus of so many admiring eyes.

'She has plenty of time to learn if she really means it,' Julia said with some annoyance. 'I started at the bottom and so does everyone!'

'I think she is dazzled by you,' Luc said quietly. 'She does not realise that you are exceptional and that she will not necessarily attain your standards!'

'I'm merely a nurse!' Julia said in exasperation. 'She could easily do anything she wanted. Nurses are always needed. Why, her English is excellent, she could train in England.'

'And who would care for her, may I ask?' Luc remarked with a wry smile at Julia's flushed and angry face. It infuriated her.

'She could live with me! She would be welcome at our house. I could help her with her exams.'

'How very rash, Sister Redford,' Luc said softly, his dark eyes amused and sardonic. 'You do not know our little Maryse, she is a handful of trouble!'

'She is a very good girl, Luc!' Lucille remonstrated softly, eyes on Maryse whose face was beginning to show signs of mutiny.

'She is near perfect,' Luc agreed quietly, his arm coming around his half-sister's tight shoulders, 'but I sometimes wonder if that is because I am near her!'

The general laughter in which Maryse joined as willingly as anyone only served to puzzle Julia. What was there here to cause a child to make a decision to remain silent? They were all fond of each other, and there was no doubt whatever that Justine was greatly loved. She felt very much superfluous to requirements and seriously doubted if she had been needed at all. Only Justine's plea, so demandingly backed by Luc, had brought her here and she had no doubt that very soon, within the next few days, it would become apparent that this was merely a holiday for her and nothing more.

It was easy to talk to Lucille, and now that her temper had subsided Maryse was eager to learn about England, nursing, and how Julia had dealt with Justine. Philippe disappeared and Luc settled with a book in the big chair at the side of the room, his attention given totally to his reading.

Julia glanced at him. The thick, curling lashes were dark against his high cheekbones, his long-fingered hands brown and capable. Even now, he looked elegant, his jacket removed and slung over the arm of the chair, and Julia's eyes came to his powerful arms, a shiver running over her that was certainly not fear.

He suddenly raised his head, looking directly at her, his eyes intent on her face, until a slow flush spread over her cheeks. For a moment they became again as they had been when they sat in the car and watched the wheeling birds, their attention rapt with each other, their eyes searching each other's faces. Any amusement that had at first been in his glance drained away and he stood abruptly, throwing down his book and picking up his discarded jacket.

'Come, Julia,' he said with an unexpected softness in his voice. 'You must be tired. It has been a long day for you and the ladies appear to be questioning you very vigorously. I will walk in the garden with you for five minutes and then show you to your room.'

'Are you sending her to bed?' Maryse asked with an astonished laugh. 'Not more than half an hour ago you were insisting that she was capable and skilful, now you treat her as a child. I have not finished talking to her. It is fascinating!'

'She will fascinate you tomorrow,' Luc said determinedly. 'Do not forget that she is our guest and would not feel able simply to walk off to bed. I know your ability to keep on talking!'

It was all taken with a laugh and Julia found herself escorted from the room whether she had wanted to go or not.

It was still warm, the night breeze soft and soothing, and Julia was glad of the darkness. Luc Marchal was a very disturbing man, far too sure of his own masculinity and far too powerful for her now that she had cast aside her own role to come here under his care.

'What is it about me, I wonder, that frightens you?' he murmured as he walked beside her. 'You have faced many things with great courage and yet you cannot face me.'

'I am facing you, *monsieur*,' she said quietly, mesmerised by him and not wishing to show it at all.

'But not with courage,' he assured her softly, his hand coming to her arm as she stumbled in the dim light. 'You still suspect that Justine fears me?'

'No!' Julia said determinedly. 'I have no idea why Justine suddenly decided to remain silent, but I'm fairly sure that it was a decision and not any other thing.'

'I agree!' he said deeply. 'You have found nothing here yet that would lead you to believe she was afraid to come home?'

'No. Everyone is charming. They love her,' Julia said quickly and he laughed softly, his grip tightening imperceptibly.

'I hope that I am included in the general charm? No doubt as time goes on you will discover what she fears. If she is ever going to tell anyone, it will obviously be you.'

'Time cannot go on for very long,' Julia reminded him, her heart suddenly accelerating at his tone, the feeling of being trapped coming back with a rush. 'I have a career and a home of my own. My father needs me, too.'

'But we all need you, Julia!' he taunted. 'You will have to decide exactly who has the greater need. Is this what alarms you, this feeling of being pulled in two directions? You are not captured. Say the word and I will take you back to England at once, this very night even, if you so decide.'

'You're making me feel rather childish!' Julia snapped. 'When I decide to make a run for it, I'll let you know!'

His quiet laughter had a strange effect on her. It was neither patronising nor unkind but it was very secret, as if he knew so many things that she did not. She was glad to plead tiredness and escape to her room.

During the next few days, Julia settled into the household, a little unsure of what to do at first. For the first couple of weeks there was to be no tutor for Justine and so they were constantly together roaming the more accessible parts of the ranch, Justine fascinated by Julia's painting and only a little fretful when Julia insisted that she have a rest each afternoon.

As to Luc, he was busy from morning until night and it suited Julia very well. When those imperious, dark eyes rested on her she was instantly thrown into confusion and unease, a strange, empty feeling hitting the pit of her stomach that she strove to control, but never quite managed. He left her well alone and was merely polite and pleasant, involved with discussions about the *manade* with Philippe at dinner and then heading for his study until bedtime.

There were many acres of land to supervise, the herds to tend, and more often than not she was awakened early in the morning as Luc and Philippe drove off in the Land Rover to the outlying parts of the ranch. Almost always she sprang out of bed to watch them go, her eyes unwillingly lingering on Luc until they were out of sight.

The evenings would have been very empty had it not been for Maryse, who sat close to Julia all the time and wanted to speak of nothing but England and nursing. Both subjects were safe and ignored by Luc. Apparently the crisis with the gentleman at the bank was past. Maryse was never late again.

'Do you realise how very clever you are?' Philippe came silently up to Julia when she was painting in the garden one afternoon, having put Justine safely to bed for a couple of hours. 'Beautiful, a skilled nurse, a talented painter. I could wish that, like Justine, I had a nurse with the face of an angel.'

'You're a little old for that,' Julia countered with a smile, glad that his tone was merely bantering. 'I thought you were out with the *gardians* today.'

'*Please, mademoiselle!* You sound like my unbending brother. I do not intend to join them until after three.

There is a drive and by then Luc will be here. He has been busy all morning and so have I. It is now time for my break and if I do not get it he will be here to drive me also before I have caught my breath. I am not at all sure that he is human. Perhaps he is like the bulls, merely single-minded!'

Philippe sank to the ground beside her, grimacing amusingly.

'I rarely have the chance to speak to you. You may take pity on me!'

'You can speak to me whenever you like,' Julia said firmly, her delicate face flushing at the mention of Luc, try as she might to hide it. 'So long as nothing interferes with my time with Justine, I'm free to do as I wish!'

'Then do you wish to dine with me one evening this week, alone? There is a small, insignificant restaurant in the nearest town. The food is good and it is quiet.' Philippe smiled into her deep blue eyes and took her hand.

'I...'

She was spared the necessity of a reply by the taunting voice that interrupted. 'You have retired from a working life, Philippe?' Luc asked in amusement, coming on them silently and towering over them both. Dressed as a *gardian*, in tight moleskin trousers, high boots and a brightly printed shirt, a wide-brimmed, flat-topped hat pushed to the back of his dark head, he looked so unlike the man who had come to England with his niece that Julia stared at him in fascination, unable to look away. Every last vestige of the suave, wealthy businessman was gone. He looked like a man of his own people, and his attitude was lighter than she had ever seen it before.

'I haven't even ordered my coffee yet!' Philippe protested, looking up at Luc without much hope. 'I thought I had captured Julia alone. There is a great deal of the spoil-sport in you, *mon ami*!'

'We have a while,' Luc said with a laugh, flinging himself down beside Julia. 'I have saddled up for you, as a matter of fact. That being the case, you may go and order coffee for Julia and me. My task was the harder!'

Philippe left with much good-natured grumbling and Julia tried to remain utterly normal, reminding herself with some irritation that she was rapidly forgetting what normal was. Every time she saw Luc now, her heart just took off at an alarming rate, and it was quite ridiculous. He was absolutely nothing to her and had never once given her reason to imagine otherwise. Except for the odd look that might well have been her own imagination, he was as he had ever been. He was much softer now, of course, but then why not? He was home, Justine returning more to her old ways every day.

'Your painting is improving rapidly, do you realise that?' he said quietly, moving closer to look at her work. 'You are beginning to be tanned and healthy-looking too. Your time here is clearly good for you.'

'My time is supposed to be good for Justine!' Julia said a little more sharply than she had intended. 'I must soon think about going home.'

'Must you spoil my days with threats?' Luc said good-humouredly. 'You have done so much for Justine and for me, am I not allowed to give you a holiday?'

'If that's why you want me to stay, then...' Julia began in surprise, but he interrupted quietly, his eyes on her face.

'If you would relax from this starchy hospital manner then you would suddenly find a very good reason why I want you to stay,' he said softly.

She had no time either to think that one out or even to reply. Philippe appeared, a newcomer with him, a vibrantly pretty girl who flung herself at Luc as he stood politely.

'You are back and I have never seen you until now, *chéri*!' she cried, her arms around his neck. 'Why have you not been to see me?'

'I have been snowed under with work!' Luc protested laughingly, his arms tightening around her. 'It is a long way to your estate. I would have come sooner or later.'

'Later, I think!' the girl laughed, her eyes brightly inquisitive as she stepped away from his arms and looked at Julia.

'Julia Redford,' Philippe introduced as it became apparent that Luc was not about to. 'Sister Redford!' he added pointedly.

'Ah yes! The nurse who has saved Justine! I met Lucille the other day and she told me about you. The family are very grateful, Sister Redford!'

Suddenly, Julia had no doubt about this girl's place in the family. Her greeting of Luc and his readiness to hold her spoke volumes, and Philippe seemed to be intent on reading her mind by the look of him. She pulled herself out of an unexpected feeling of dismay and smiled brightly as Philippe continued the introductions.

'This is Rosanne Dupin, Julia,' he said with a smile. 'She lives on the next estate, but far enough away to keep her out of our hair for most of the time.'

'I have come to help with the drive!' Rosanne protested. 'We completed ours yesterday and, not knowing that Luc was here I thought I would give you a hand.'

'Then bring your coffee and I will saddle up for you,' Philippe said determinedly.

'Will Mademoiselle Redford ride with us?' Rosanne said, her smile a little stiff as Luc once more sat beside Julia. 'Can you ride, *mademoiselle*?'

'Even if she can, she will not ride with us to move the bulls!' Luc said determinedly. 'She is valuable in her own right being exactly what she is. Julia is not here to be a *gardian*!'

'I want her all in one piece for tonight, in any câse,' Philippe put in swiftly, smiling at Julia. 'She is dining with me in town.'

It was news to Julia. She had not agreed at all, but it now seemed to be a very good idea and she smiled back readily.

'We will all go together,' Luc said firmly. 'We will collect Rosanne on the way.'

Philippe looked a little taken aback but he accepted it with his usual good nature and Rosanne looked very pleased with herself. She was more ready to go along with Philippe and leave Luc here now that he was taking her out tonight, and Julia did not know what to say to Luc when they had gone laughing and joking towards the stables.

'You do not mind that Rosanne and I are joining you on your date?' Luc said quietly.

'It's hardly a date!' Julia reminded him a little sharply.

'That is a pity,' he murmured softly. 'It is time that you forgot about this doctor of yours. Philippe is good company, as you will see.'

His ready acceptance of this dismayed Julia more than she had believed possible and she had to remind herself sharply that she was only here for a while, that it was merely because of their anxieties about Justine that she was here at all.

'I'd better get Justine up or she'll never sleep tonight,' Julia said quickly, standing and gathering her things.

Luc stood too, bending to help her, his hand lingering as he handed her the paints that she had used.

'I hope you do not think that we are cutting you out of things by leaving you here as we go on the drive,' he said, looking at her intently. 'It is sometimes a little dangerous. Rosanne is used to such things, but you are not.'

'I have Justine to see to,' Julia reminded him, making herself face those dark and probing eyes. 'I hope I didn't give the impression that I was displeased.'

'Displeased, no. But there is suddenly a little sadness in you, is there not?' he enquired astutely. 'I wish you to be happy here.'

'How could I not be?' Julia asked, her eyes lowered as she gave up the attempt to face him out. 'I can paint. Justine is a delight. It's like a holiday.'

'A very long one, I hope!' he said softly. He took her hand, raising it to his lips. '*Alors!* If you are reasonably happy then I will go. *A bientôt, Julia!*' He strode off to join the other two and Julia felt shaken at the reaction she had to this small act of contact. Surely she had faced misery enough? Was she once again throwing herself so deeply into her feelings, her love of life, that she would be distraught to leave this dark and unusual man?

The meal out had been a mistake. She acknowledged that almost as soon as they were settled to dine at the small local restaurant. With only Philippe here she would have enjoyed it. There was the opportunity to watch the people of the Camargue, the *gardians* dressed up for the evening who greeted Luc with a great deal of respect and Philippe as one of themselves. Rosanne, however, was making it more than clear that this was not just a casual foursome. Very pointedly she let it be known that she was with Luc and, although he took it in his stride easily, Philippe was not his usual smiling self.

Again and again Julia's eyes were drawn to Luc. It was an act that was completely against her will. There was a dreadful feeling of inevitability about being close to Luc Marchal. There had been this feeling from the first, and she was terrified that he would realise it.

Her own inner agitation only served to make things worse, and by the time they were ready to leave, Julia was wishing herself miles away. Her dismay grew when a close neighbour of Rosanne's who had joined them with his wife towards the end of the meal suggested that they run Rosanne home, saving Luc the journey. Philippe, to her astonishment, intervened to say that he would take her as he had some business to discuss with her father about the coming sales.

She found herself alone with Luc, and he did not look too pleased about it.

'I would have thought that you would be the one to discuss such things with Monsieur Dupin,' Julia ventured as they drove off.

'And why would you think that?' he said darkly. 'One day, Philippe will run a *manade* of his own, the one where we now live, as a matter of fact. I have my own place and, when he is quite ready to take over, I shall move out. I have enough to do without running two ranches.'

'Oh! I didn't know that!' Julia confessed quickly, her mind searching through this new information. Would he take Justine with him? Would he marry Rosanne and then look after Justine as his own child? They were certainly close. He could hardly leave her behind.

'I—I suppose you have plans for then…I mean about settling down and that sort of thing?' she said a little unwisely.

'I usually do have plans,' he said quietly, turning to look at her. 'What particular plan did you have in mind, *mademoiselle*?'

For no reason he was a little angry, and his cool, sardonic voice quite silenced her. When she did not reply, he stopped the car suddenly, turning to stare at her. It was dark and silent and she felt a great rush of emotion, making her feel only weakness and a sudden tearfulness that was quite inexplicable.

They sat quite still, their eyes locked and Luc's dark forehead creased in a frown. His gaze moved to her lips that trembled just a little and then to the frantically beating pulse in the soft hollow of her neck before moving back to capture her worried blue eyes.

'What plans?' he asked intently. 'You are once again searching for a truth, a reason. What is it now? You imagine that Justine is afraid that I will leave her? Once again I am the villain?'

'I never thought that!' Julia said with an attempt to return to her old attitude with him, but it failed. She was trembling too much for that. Her words came out more like a plea and his attention sharpened.

'It is not a good idea,' he muttered, almost angrily, and Julia was so much afraid of her own feelings that she could not ask what he meant.

The hard, strong hand captured her chin, tilting her face.

'Twice in your life to my certain knowledge you have been badly hurt,' he murmured. 'It is not a good idea to invite further hurt, further damage!'

'I don't know what you mean.' She could only manage a whisper with those compelling eyes holding her in bondage, and he shook his head angrily, his grip tightening.

'Perhaps you do not but I suspect that you do. You are quite transparent sometimes and at others you are a mystery to me. One thing I do know, however; I want you around. I do not look forward to seeing Justine's face when you tell her that you are about to leave!'

'I can't just go on staying here!' Julia protested in a low voice, and he smiled slowly, his hand drawing her forward.

'Then I will have to try and persuade you, Julia,' he said in a voice suddenly roughened.

His lips caught hers, startling her for only a moment, and, though it was the first time, she knew that she had been waiting for this for days, perhaps even weeks. It was not a particularly gentle kiss but her body softened in response, her lips opening, her arms immediately encircling his neck.

It surprised him. She felt shock waves right through him and for a second he moved to leave her, but his heart was hammering over her own, and whatever chivalrous instinct had made him momentarily withdraw, he quelled it and moved in closer to lift her into his arms and deepen the kiss.

She was dazed when he lifted his head, his hand still cupping her face, his arm holding her tightly.

'I am rarely taken by surprise,' he murmured. 'I expected a fight from you. You are lonely now that this doctor has left you? Is that why you are so ready for me?'

'I'm not!' Shame flooded over her and she struggled very belatedly.

'*Dieu*, but you are!' he ground out. 'Would Philippe have done equally well?' Her hand freed itself and rose to lash out at him but he caught it and held it fast against his chest.

'So! Now we know then, *mademoiselle*,' he said softly. 'I have overstepped the bounds of hospitality, but you needed that kiss as much as I!'

'Take me back!' Julia snapped, her legs trembling as she sat bolt upright in the car. 'If you ever touch me again, I'll go straight home in spite of Justine!'

'I think not, Julia,' he said quietly, starting the car and pulling away. 'I told you, did I not, that I would alter your life? I did not then realise how very much I would alter it, but we have not finished our discussion by any means.'

CHAPTER SIX

THE screams woke her, the screams and the shouting, and at first she thought that they were coming from her own lips. Her dreams had been disturbed, Lucy, Justine and Luc walking darkly through them, her own protesting spirit agonised at their presence, but the screams continued, the shouting increased and she was out of bed at once, racing into the passage, hastily tying her robe around her.

'*Non!* It's not true! It's not true! Stop it! Stop it!'

Justine's voice was pitched at hysterical level and Julia recognised the dangerous sound, so damaging for the child.

The passage seemed to be filled with people in various states of dress, and as Julia ran into Justine's room she saw Luc trying to calm the child. Justine was awake now but clearly the nightmare was not over. Whatever had walked through her dreams haunted her still and she was resisting all Luc's efforts to calm her, unwilling it seemed to have him close at all.

'Julia! Julia!'

As her eyes fell on Julia she held out her arms and Luc moved aside, standing to watch sombrely as Julia gathered the distraught child to her.

'There now, it's only a dream. Now it's quite gone!' Julia rocked her gently, her voice soothing, but Justine was stiff and afraid, her face buried against Julia's shoulder, her hands clutching tightly.

It was with a small shiver of alarm that Julia realised the little girl was whispering, so low that the words were quite inaudible. Her eyes met Luc's and he understood quickly that Justine meant to say something for Julia's ears alone.

'We must leave her to Julia,' he said quietly to the others who now crowded worriedly into the room. 'It is quite plain that she wants no one else. I think it would be a good idea if you were all to go back to bed. I will make Justine a milky drink and no doubt Julia will have calmed her by then.'

They accepted it with no question and soon the room was silent, the door closed and Justine raised a tear-stained face.

'She killed my papa, Julia! It was all my fault! *Maman* tried to kill us all, because of me!'

'Hush, hush! It was an accident. Everyone knows that, darling!'

Julia rocked her quietly, hearing the small sobs lessen, feeling the clutching hands hold less tightly.

'*Non!* It was not an accident. They do not know! She killed him and *Oncle* Luc must not find out!'

He came in at that moment, a glass of warm milk in his hand, but Justine avoided his eyes, only accepting the drink when Julia handed it to her, agitated again until Luc looked at Julia and walked from the room.

He was outside the door when Julia eventually managed to settle Justine and came out on to the passage.

'Come downstairs,' he suggested quietly. 'I will make a drink for both of us. You look a trifle shaken, and I cannot say that I feel deliriously happy at this turn of events.'

Julia followed him without any thought, Justine's words still ringing in her mind. What imagined guilt did that child bear? It was not over by any means and she had been foolish to think otherwise. A mind that could decide to be silent was troubled deeply and she must stay here until she found out why.

'She has told you something?' Luc said with certainty as he handed her a coffee, and Julia nodded, her eyes a little wary.

'Out with it, then!' he grated. 'It concerns me, I know. There is suspicion yet again on your face! If I am a villain I would like to know about it!'

Julia sat at the long, scrubbed table in the warm kitchen and faced him squarely. 'You're quite wrong,' she informed him quietly. 'If I look anything at all it is puzzled. Who was driving when the accident happened?' she suddenly asked.

'Jules!' Luc said with no hesitation, relaxing a little as he sat on the edge of the table and looked down at her. 'When they found the car, Jules was still at the wheel. There could be no question whatever that Deirdre was driving.'

'Then why does Justine insist that her mother killed her father and, in fact, tried to kill them all?' Julia asked softly, her deep blue eyes questioning on his face.

For a moment he looked astonished and then his eyes narrowed thoughtfully.

'Why did she not tell me this? As I am clearly not involved I cannot see why she would not have told me. Why should I be excluded? All her young life she has run to me when Jules was not there. She never ran to her mother. Deirdre was utterly unfeeling towards the child. Why save this for you, Julia?'

'You were wrong when you imagined that she wanted a new mother,' Julia said softly, her expression compassionate as she saw the raw look in his dark eyes. 'She has come to me because I'm a friend, that's all. She told me because I'm not involved. It's not unusual. Her last words were that you must never find out, and you must not mention this until we have the whole thing solved.'

'*I* must never find out?' Luc looked at her deeply, astonishment on his face, and she had not the slightest doubt that, no matter what Justine imagined, Luc was in no way involved.

'It seems that there is to be no end to this,' he said wearily, and Julia's heart went out to him.

'There will be,' she assured him quietly. 'We're much further forward than we were. Not too long ago, Justine would not speak at all. Now, she is beginning to tell us why. We'll get to the bottom of it, don't worry.'

In her compassion, her hand had gone out to touch his and he turned it into his strong palm, looking down at the slender fingers in the warmth of his hand.

'So you will not desert us?' he asked quietly, his dark eyes rising to search her own.

Soft colour tinted her cheeks but she stood resolutely, gently removing her hand, her eyes meeting his.

'I never leave a job half done, *monsieur*!' she said firmly, and his lips softened into a smile.

'It is hard to be Sister Redford when you are in a pretty nightdress and a silken robe, is it not? You did that rather well, though, and I am filled with admiration.' He stood, his hand tilting her determined chin. 'Tomorrow I will arrange for Justine's tutor to come. It would be better if her mind were fully occupied, do you not agree?'

'Definitely!' Julia said, a little afraid to attempt to move away in case his softened mood should end. There was something warm and intimate about being here with Luc, and she could have stayed all night simply looking at him.

'Also,' he added quietly, 'you are not a nursemaid. I am filled with guilt when I remember how I have treated you, the demands I have placed on you. I do not wish you to have to take care of Justine. I only ask that you be here, Julia, because we need you.'

'I'll stay,' Julia said softly, her eyes clinging to his in spite of her mind's urgent warnings.

'I am grateful, *ma chère*,' he assured her quietly, his eyes moving over her face, 'so grateful that I will remind myself that you have suffered much hurt. It would be best if you went now to bed. Goodnight, Julia.'

To her dismay, he turned and walked from the room and she realised that she was becoming very obvious to him, her expression too clear for him to see. Rosanne would be here more often now though and she would have to stifle her feelings for Luc if she was to stay and see Justine fully recovered. Now, she had promised! She sighed deeply and went up to her room, the house quiet and dark around her.

Things returned to normal. Justine's tutor came and much of the day was occupied with lessons. Julia was now simply a friend, and it was as a friend that Justine sought her out each day. There was time on her hands now, enough time for her to extend her painting and move out of the garden without Justine. She was always watchful, but whatever was troubling the child was now well back beneath the surface.

She had little choice but to play the game Justine's way until the secret was told and the child's fears put to rest. A routine had been established now that lessons were again progressing and Julia knew exactly when Justine would be free. She was always there, waiting, hoping for further revelations, but none were forthcoming.

Luc seemed to spend more and more time away from the ranch, only appearing at dinner time, usually unapproachable even then, and Rosanne Dupin came to dinner too with a regularity that convinced Julia that one day she would marry Luc. He was clearly fond of her and she was as well informed about the affairs of the ranching as Luc and Philippe. The after-dinner discussions now included Rosanne and Julia spend much of her after-dinner time with Maryse and Lucille, both of whom were becoming more like old friends daily.

In her free time she painted, becoming deeply immersed in the ambience of the place but never able to leave the nearer confines of the ranch house because of Justine. One day there would be a crack in the armour that the child had built around herself, and Julia wanted to be there when that happened.

She had noticed that the birds did not all stay by the *étangs*. They came to the ranch, moving in their inquisitive way about the pasture. Down by the gates at the entrance, she made herself a little 'hide', breathless with excitement when they wandered close, her skilled fingers capturing their movement, their colours and their surroundings.

Already, Justine had two brilliant pictures on her walls, an egret motionless under the tamarisk trees, a purple heron in flight against a dark, storm-threatening sky. They were good, very good, she knew that. They were the best things she had ever done and they held the mystery that she felt here, an oppressive beauty excitingly tinged with danger.

Luc had looked at her hard when Justine had excitedly shown him the gifts that Julia had painted for her room, but he had said nothing. Later, Justine had led her to her room and shown her the finished result. *Oncle* Luc had taken them to be framed and they were resplendent on the wall behind her bed, as grandly framed as old masters. She was left with the uncomfortable feeling that he had felt her anxious mood and that this expensive framing was a reward to soothe her. It was like an unspoken message, although he seemed now to keep strictly out of her way, never making any comment on her work at all.

She was glad of her hide when one day the winds that swept the Camargue were stronger than ever. Today she had longer, but she doubted if the birds would come. Justine had gone off for the whole afternoon with her grandmother, visiting friends a couple of villages away, and Julia had refused the invitation to accompany them. Justine was safe with Lucille, and she herself felt the need to unwind in the silence of her little nest by the gate.

The sound of a Land Rover stopping close by startled her out of her reverie. Vehicles went up and down the track frequently but they never stopped and she was uneasy when Luc peered in at her, his dark face quite expressionless.

'Justine is out for the day with her grandmother,' she said defensively and his black eyebrows raised mockingly.

'I know it. Do not be so ready to defend yourself. You are not a servant caught taking time off!'

'It was merely a remark! I have no reason to defend myself!'

The rapid beating of her heart threatened to choke her and he was as usual utterly dominant, peculiarly silent even though he was crouched down looking in at her. Annoyance with herself and her feelings had sharpened her voice and he muttered crossly, straightening up.

'Come out from there! I cannot see you properly, and I absolutely refuse to kneel down and peer at any woman!' He was now towering away outside and Julia crawled out, dusting off her skirt and reaching in to get her things.

'Leave them! Nobody would dare touch them. This little nest and the delights that come from it are a source of wonder to the *gardians*. I am not at all sure that they do not cross themselves as they ride by; certainly their eyes are more on this place than on the horses for most of the time!'

'It's hardly my fault!' Julia snapped, cross when he pulled her to her feet and stared down at her with cold, black eyes. 'The superstitions of the Camarguais are quite beyond me and no doubt quite stupid.'

'For one with such a wonderful face, you have a tongue like a steel file at times,' he said wryly, seemingly amused all at once. 'Get in the Land Rover and try to keep your nerve. We have not talked for some time, and at the moment I have no murderous intent although by the expression on your face one would think that I had.'

In the face of such sarcasm, she climbed stiffly into the vehicle, gathering the skirts of her sun-dress around her and trying to be calm. Maybe he wanted a companion for afternoon tea? Rosanne wouldn't like that! She blushed as a swift pang of jealousy caught her unaware, suddenly becoming conscious that he was still standing there, the door in his hand, the dark eyebrows raised sardonically. She had the decided feeling that he had read her thoughts and found them utterly amusing. She looked away and he slammed the door, coming to climb in beside her and turn the heavy vehicle in a tight circle, heading out and away from the ranch in a rush of speed that had her clinging to the seat.

'Where are we going?' She could even hear the panic in her own voice.

'Visiting, *mademoiselle*,' he assured her calmly, taking another and decidedly more bumpy road off the main road that led from the Manade de Michaud.

'I'm not dressed for visiting!' She looked down at the skirt of her dress, searching anxiously for creases, but he glanced at her sideways, a quick glance that seemed to take in everything about her.

'For this visit, you will be quite adequately dressed!'

He lapsed into his usual silence and Julia decided to do likewise. She had not had the time to prepare herself for this encounter with Luc and she realised that, every day, she prepared herself to meet him almost without knowing that she did it. She felt all the time that she was out of her depth. Since the incident in the kitchen he had almost ignored her, but the same electrical feelings were there every time they were in the same room together, and though he said nothing she knew that he felt it too.

Often she would look up and find his eyes on her, dark, burning and filled with a look closely akin to resentment. Why he had chosen to come for her this afternoon she had no idea. Avoiding her would have been the best solution it seemed. Even now, he obviously had not the faintest desire to speak to her. She was angry with herself and childishly angry with him.

They entered a lonely road, passing a solitary *gardian's* hut close to the entrance, and drove along the long track that seemed to be leading to another *manade*. The horses were there too, even more of them, the ferny tamarisk trees, the marsh sampire, but the place was wilder, lonelier and oddly more beautiful.

The white-walled ranch house stood among lawns, the gardens carefully tended, and Julia caught her breath as a white heron, motionless as a statue on the lawn, suddenly swept upwards into the still sky. Luc stopped the engine and there was silence, utter stillness an almost frightening peace as they both sat looking at the house.

'It—it's so quiet!' Julia found herself whispering and he glanced across at her quickly.

'That worries you?'

'No! It's quite beautiful. Who lives here?'

'I do! Or at least, very soon, I intend to live here, when Philippe can shoulder his responsibilities and his inheritance. I will then be free to follow my own inclinations, and my inclination is to live here.'

He grinned, suddenly a different person, and then turned to leap out, slamming the driver's door loudly and coming round to her side. 'Come then, *mademoiselle*! Let us make a little noise and frighten the devil away!' He reached up and caught her by the waist, lifting her out and setting her on her feet before she could catch her breath.

The hall was wide and well lit, dark, old beams telling of great age, and the walls were lined with oil paintings of bulls, great, black, fierce-looking brutes, each named.

'The great breeding bulls of the past that founded my family's fortune!' he said with a sweep of his hand. 'I tell you this hastily in case you think that they are my ancestors!' He was suddenly laughing and took her hand light-heartedly, leading her into the wide and spacious salon that only needed a woman's touch to make it perfect. Julia stood entranced, her eyes darting everywhere, and his laughing voice behind her made her blush wildly, considering the thoughts that had been racing through her mind.

'Alter it all you wish, provided that it is merely mental speculation, *mademoiselle*,' he said in amusement, smiling into her rosy face and then leading her round the rest of the house. It was difficult not to begin her mental rearrangements in every room, and he knew quite well the struggle she was having.

'Well? Tell me what you think of it and then you will be rewarded,' he said as they were once again in the salon. 'I will make coffee for you myself.'

'Is—isn't there anyone here?' It was a particularly stupid thing to say, as she knew perfectly well that they were alone.

'I am here and you are here.' He was suddenly not amused any more and she wished she had not spoken at all.

'Why—why did you bring me here?' She turned away, walking towards the window, very anxious now to be gone.

'I brought you to show you my home, my *own* home, where I will live for the rest of my life. I thought it might interest you. You are very interested in many things.'

'Of course! The Camargue is a fascinating place and you've got a lot of land. One day, I may come back and look at the whole Camargue!'

'You are not again contemplating an early departure, I hope?' he asked quietly, a hint of steel behind the softly spoken words.

'No, but I can't just go on staying here, you know that! I have a job of my own! I—I don't talk about it but I miss it, and my father.'

'I am unfair to you, am I not?' he asked with a suddenly sombre note in his voice. 'I ask of you things that I have no right to ask: your time, your patience, your compassion. Even now I have dragged you here away from the thing that you enjoy doing!'

'I'm happy to be here!' Julia said quickly, turning towards him. 'I told you I'm fascinated with the Camargue. This is a beautiful house, a bit lonely, but then I don't suppose you'll mind that when you're married!'

'Ah! You are now arranging my life for me as you once accused me of arranging yours!'

'Of course not!' Julia turned her back and looked out of the window again, her tongue running wildly on. 'It's just so obvious that you'll need a wife, and as you're a landowner I imagine that Rosanne's inheritance would make your own into almost a small empire.'

'It would!' he agreed, making her heart sink.

He came closer, standing behind her, and there was a certain amount of panic in her voice when she started to turn away.

'We'd better be going!' she said sharply. 'It was nice of you to let me see your house, but rather a long way to come.'

'I imagined that it would be worth it,' he said quietly, his hands coming to span her waist, drawing her back to him. 'I brought you here because we are alone here, not to see my house!' He caught her shoulders and spun her round, almost lifting her off her feet and bringing her close to the hard-packed strength of his body. 'I cannot continue to look at you and not touch!'

His arm tightly came around her, his other hand speared in her hair, he lifted her face to his, no escape possible.

'It is clear that I must decide about you. I am not a man who can be teased. You have stopped saying that you will leave until today but it is always on your face, and I expect almost daily to be faced with your departure. Meanwhile, I work myself to death to avoid you. Perhaps I can rid myself of the feelings that boil inside me every time I see you!'

He was angry with himself and Julia tensed as his lips closed harshly over hers, the strong arms like a steel prison.

'Luc!' Her cry, almost crushed beneath his lips, had him raising his head, his eyes burning darkly.

'Shh! Hush, Julia,' he said roughly against her lips. 'You know that we want each other!'

Her lips parted beneath his and this time he did not let her go; he allowed his own feelings to flare out of control, a dangerous experiment, and they both sensed the danger as his fire caught her too and her arms went around his neck. It was an explosion of feeling long hidden, well controlled, and instantly she was closer, pressed to the length of him, his hard hands urging her closer.

'Julia!' Her name was a hoarse cry on his lips as he covered her face and neck with kisses, his mouth burning her shoulders as the straps of her sun-dress were ruthlessly pushed aside.

He suddenly swept her up into his arms, striding to the settee and placing her on the cushions, coming down to her at once, his hard body covering hers, every inch of him demanding.

'Luc! I'm afraid!' she gasped out, holding him off with trembling hands, and he drew back to look at her, his harshly handsome face taut with desire, before his expression softened.

'Yes, I can see that you are,' he murmured softly. 'Come!'

He did not intend to let her go, but his hands softened, his whole demeanour changed magically, and the irresistible tenderness of his touch had her sighing in his arms within minutes as he coaxed the tension from her and stilled her fears, leaving her prey to every emotion inside her.

The lips that roamed over her were like velvet, the words that he murmured were heated and soft, and Julia gave herself up to the fondling hands with no thought but delight, gasping with pleasure as his hands peeled the sun-dress to her waist and his lips urged the tips of her breasts to sharp excitement.

'*Tu n'as pas peur de moi, chérie?*' he murmured, his hands capturing the swollen beauty of her breasts.

'No, I'm not afraid!' She was desperately anxious that he should not stop and his dark eyes met hers at the sharp anxiety in her voice, his intake of breath swift and harsh at the expression on her face.

'*Viens, ma belle!*' he breathed harshly, lifting her towards him. 'You and I are like fire in the dry grasses, *tu comprends*? Whenever I see you I wish to be here with you, like this!'

And she felt like fire, like a wild flame, rising to meet every hard movement of his body, totally lost in the suspended time in this wild place. It was the thought of the place that froze her in his arms, the thought of Rosanne. Graham had wanted her too, still wanted her but not as his wife. Rosanne would be Luc's wife, their land joined, both of them Camarguais. Hadn't she seen the way they had their heads together, Philippe, Luc and Rosanne, all understanding each other? She was the outsider, a passing passion for Luc.

She stiffened, turning her head aside, rejection in the whole of her attitude, and his eyes narrowed on her face as he drew back to look at her. For a moment he said nothing, straightening her dress and pulling her to her feet to stand looking at her with cool considering eyes.

'You do not trust well, do you, Julia?' he asked in a taut voice. 'Deep inside you there is this belief that I am responsible for Justine's problems, and now you believe that I intend to seduce you before returning you to your father. I suppose you have not recovered from the love you had for this worthless doctor. You are not yet again a woman, although you look at me with a woman's eyes, a woman's desire. Fear not, *ma chère*, I had intended to take you back before things went too far!'

It brought her into the present, back into her own character and the realisation of where this had been leading, her sheltered mind and upbringing shocked and shaken that she could have allowed herself to be here with Luc when she knew very well what his future held.

'I—I wouldn't have...'

'You would had I continued!' He looked at her calmly, totally in control of himself with alarming speed. 'In spite of your doctor fiancé, you are naïve and as unaware of your own passions as a child. Passions run high in the Camargue. I will take you home.'

'It's not my home!' Julia said wildly, her face flushed and beautiful. 'I live in England, and now of course, I must go back at once!'

'I think not, Julia!' he said shortly, leading her to the door and out into the gathering dusk. 'You will stay for Justine because you cannot let things go. You are a perfectionist and Justine is not cured. The nurse in you is ever uppermost, the woman afraid and unsure. I could make you stay—for me!'

'Don't fool yourself!' Julia snapped, trying to pull away.

'I rarely do,' he bit out angrily, taking her bodily and lifting her with ease into the Land Rover. 'And in this case, I am not fooling myself at all. Any time that I reach for you, you will come to me, but you are not Camarguais and you are a guest in my house!'

That said it all and he was as silent on the drive back as he had been coming. The experiment was over.

It was a relief to see Lucille arriving with an excited Justine as they stopped in front of the Manade de Michaud.

'I have eaten already!' Justine cried, leaping from the car and racing round to Luc as he climbed from the bigger Land Rover. 'I had mullet, asparagus, rice and strawberries! I ate every last bit!'

'You will be fatter than a duck!' Luc swung her up into his arms, hugging her to him, and Julia suddenly had a picture of him with his own child, some dark haired boy or girl with the stamp of the Camargue on them. It brought tears to the back of her eyes and she knew that in his arms she had admitted to herself a love so wild and strong that she could not yet fully believe it. The love she had imagined with Graham was shallow and brittle but the way she felt about Luc was burning and deep, a passion that she had not known herself to be capable of. She raced off to her room, changing for dinner quickly, greatly pleased when the tap on her door was from Justine and nobody else.

'Will you help me to bed, Julia?' Justine coaxed with a rare grin. 'I am tired and very full.'

'You'll be totally better any day now,' Julia said as she sat on the bed later and looked at the little girl, so frail when she had first seen her but now so much stronger. 'I'll be able to go home then.'

'Oh, no!' Justine instantly clasped her hands and held on tightly. '*Oncle* Luc will not let you go! He said that while I want you here you will stay, and I want you here for ever!'

Such faith in *Oncle* Luc's dominance! Julia tried to laugh but it was hard, and already the small, pretty face was clouded with sleepiness.

'We'll see,' she added soothingly and Justine smiled sleepily, her eyes already closed.

'I like it when you say that. It means good things. I am happy when you are here, Julia. One day, everything will be all right and *Oncle* Luc will take care of both of us!'

CHAPTER SEVEN

IN SPITE of everything, Julia was surprised to find Philippe arriving early next day with a small Renault which he parked with a flourish. He beckoned to her, grinning all over his face.

'Now I am useful merely as a delivery boy!' he said as she came outside and looked at him suspiciously. 'Do not be so anxious, Julia. Big brother has sent this along for you. He says that you are too restricted here and the use of this will make it possible for you to travel further afield when you paint this noble land.'

'I—I'm astonished!' Julia walked around the bright yellow little car. 'Are you quite sure, Philippe? This is not one of your odd jokes that's going to get me into trouble?'

'Word of honour!' He crossed his heart and grinned at her, his head on one side as he regarded her startled face. 'In any case, it is not possible to get you into trouble with Luc; he would rather blame anyone else no matter what you did.'

'Little do you know!' Julia said darkly, adding hastily at the speculating look in his eyes. 'In any case, he never notices that I paint, I'm sure.'

'Oh, no?' Philippe said with friendly sarcasm. 'That must be why he goes for miles to get the frames!'

'That was for Justine! Anyway, thank you very much for delivering it. I'll thank Luc when I see him.'

It was time to dismiss Philippe, she thought. He was always ready to flirt, and another clash with Luc was the last thing she wanted.

Justine was delighted.

'Oh, how kind he is! Do you not agree, Julia, that he is the kindest man in the whole world?'

'I'm sure he must be,' Julia murmured, certainly he was just about the strangest! 'This afternoon, we will go to the Etang de Vaccarès and look at the flamingoes.'

It quite made Justine's day and Julia had to admit that it had made hers; not only because she did not now feel quite so trapped but because Luc had been thinking about her. She got the chance to thank him at dinner time after a long, hot afternoon watching the wheeling and landing of the flame-bright flamingoes. Their movements, their colours were still in her mind, and it was with shining eyes that she approached Luc in the salon before dinner.

'I want to thank you for the car, Luc,' she said softly. 'It was very kind of you to think about it. Even today, it's made such a difference to me.'

'And you have been watching the flamingoes!' he said with a half-smile on his lips.

'Well, yes! How did you know?'

'The English nose is a little red, a little touched by the sun,' he said with a smile. He ran his long finger down the length of her profile, a subtle movement that was almost a caress, and Julia's shivering reaction brought the same sparks to the back of his dark eyes. 'I will have to get you a large floppy hat,' he added softly, his eyes holding hers.

'Luc can be very indulgent,' Rosanne said sharply, coming close and sliding her arm into Luc's possessively.

'When he wants!' Luc finished for her sardonically and the moment had gone, the dark spell was broken. A wordless protest flared across Julia's face, the shine dying from her eyes, and Luc looked at her with narrowed gaze for a second before turning abruptly away. 'Let us eat!' he said harshly. 'I have a lot to do this evening and so has Philippe, so the ladies will have to be left to themselves.'

After that she saw little of Luc. Much of her time with Justine was spent away from the *manade* as they explored the villages and the surrounding countryside together, and her paintings grew, subtly changing as she absorbed the mystery of the Camargue. She could even see it herself. She was changed in so many ways. She was more mature, saddened in an entirely different way, almost wildly in love with a hard, dark man who would eventually marry someone else.

The thought of returning to England and putting an end to this daily torture was ever present in her mind, but she put off the day. If she left and Justine deteriorated, Luc would only call her back. And she would come, there was no doubt of that, she would leave everything to come.

She was going out one afternoon when Rosanne arrived. She seemed to haunt the place and, try as she might, Julia could not stifle the jealousy she felt for the girl.

'I've seen the paintings you do. You're very good,' Rosanne said with a smile. 'Why do you always do birds and flowers?'

'I suppose it's because I do them best,' Julia replied, surprised by this sudden friendliness.

'You would make a very good painting of the white horses, I think,' Rosanne said with a great deal of enthusiasm. 'Your style is so flowing. I can even see the finished picture in my head!'

'They don't stand still for long,' Julia mused, the idea suddenly seeming very good. 'I'd like to paint them but not in large numbers, not grazing close to the house like any other horses.'

'On the *étangs*!' Rosanne agreed eagerly. 'There is a place not too far away where they are always to be found. Now that Luc has given you a car you could easily drive there. It is a great, flooded stretch of plain and the horses splash around there. You would be able to work well!'

It seemed to be a good idea and Rosanne gave very careful instructions. Perhaps she wanted her out of the way more, Julia thought; she was usually very watchful when Luc and Philippe were there. In any case, Julia wanted to go. Something new might take her mind off Luc. If it were not for Justine she would go home now! Even as she thought it she felt a wave of panic. She could no more leave Luc than she could leave Justine. She saw little of him now, but life without a sight of him would be utterly empty. It was a chastening thought considering Rosanne and her obvious attachment to him, and Julia drove out to the place where the horses were supposed to be, her mind turning over the new hurt that she was slowly building inside her.

It was a desolate, empty place with a wild beauty of its own that a few brief weeks ago she would have shunned as too lonely, almost forsaken. Now though with the sky above her and the stretch of water before her she could see what these people saw. She was beginning to look at things through the eyes of a Camarguais. It would help little, though, because she was an outsider, a stranger in this land.

She stopped the bright yellow car at the side of the road and looked out across the water. Sure enough there were horses, three or four of them, but they were some distance away and in the wrong place for the light.

Julia stepped from the car and went to the water's edge. If she could get a little closer she could make her preliminary sketches and then do a great deal from memory but there was no way of going in there except on foot, and she did not fancy stepping in and then sinking to her waist.

It looked shallow enough though for a few yards from the roadside and she took off her shoes, leaving them in the car, and gingerly stepped into the water. It was not as cold as she had anticipated and by taking care she was able to get quite a way from the road, warily approaching the horses who raised their heads and looked in her direction from time to time but largely ignored her.

Her pencil flew along. It was a precarious position but she was completely absorbed in a very short while, the scene growing beneath her fingers with a talent that she had not before fully realised. The horses too were most obliging, keeping quite still for most of the time, and there was an almost uncanny silence about the place.

Suddenly, the whole scene changed! The horses who seconds before had almost been posing for her threw up their heads and then wheeled, racing away at high speed, water splashing around them, and she was left almost open-mouthed at the change, wondering how on earth she could have startled them, when she had not even made a move.

The growing sound though soon told her that they had not been concerned about her lowly presence; others were coming and coming fast. First, she heard the thunder of noise, a noise that grew even louder, and sharp cries carried over the water, the combination quite terrifying, and then the heads of the first horses appeared, the forerunners of the herd.

She realised that she was standing calf-deep in water, in front of a racing herd of wild and semi-wild horses who were being driven towards her. Of all the days she could have chosen, this was the one when she should not have been here. Rosanne's specific instructions, her insistence, the look on her face came into Julia's mind, and then she was absorbed only with the thought of survival.

They seemed to be upon her with uncanny speed. They were being driven line abreast, the *gardians* running them hard, each man seeming to be part of the white horse he rode. Flat black hats pulled well down over their eyes, tridents in hand, they were magnificent, unreal and terrifying.

She was stunned into inaction, caught in a nightmare of flashing hooves, flying spray, gleaming coats and bared teeth with occasional glimpses of hard, dark riders like horsemen from another world.

And as she stood there motionless, simply unable to move from their path, one dark figure seemed to leap out at her, his horse moving with frightening speed to overtake the leaders of the herd and outstrip them.

'Yah! Ay—yah! Yah!' Waving his hat, his trident jabbing menacingly at their heads, by some miracle he turned them, slewing away as they thundered to the distant haze of sky and water, and then he was upon her, leaping from his horse, water splashing to his knees and over the high black boots as he grasped her shoulders and shook her hard like a lifeless doll.

'Imbécile!'

There was a fury on Luc's dark face that she had never seen before. His hat was lost and his black hair was tousled across his angry face. The fingers that bit into her shoulders were like hot steel and he seemed to have lost control of his temper with no hope of recovery.

'Did I buy you a car for this, so that you could come out here and almost kill yourself?' he roared. 'Where is your much-vaunted common sense? You are as useless as a child!'

'You—you *bought* the car just for me?' It was the only thought that seemed to stick in her head and earned her another hard shake.

'Stop talking stupidly! *Dieu!* I could kill you myself! Why did you stand there like a glassy-eyed doll? Where is your instinct for self-preservation? Did you father restore Justine to me so that I could feel free to kill his only daughter?' He let her go abruptly, as if unable to be certain that he would not harm her in his rage. 'Answer me!'

Julia looked wildly at him and then her legs gave out utterly and she fell at his feet into the water, so shaken that her whole body trembled uncontrollably.

When he picked her up she was soaked to the skin, water dripping from her hair, the sketch floating away on the very waves she herself had created, and to her astonishment he reached forward and scooped it up before turning back to the road and the safe haven of the small car.

'I will take you back. We are both soaked and clearly you have been badly shocked,' he muttered, putting her into the passenger seat and striding round to fold his great length behind the wheel.

'I—I can manage,' she whispered, certain that this new discomfort would merely enrage him more. However, he seemed to have regained some measure of control over that wild temper.

'I think not!' He did not look at her but started the car at once and proceeded to pull away.

'Your horse...!' She looked back over her shoulder and the white horse was still where he had left it, standing obediently, and who would not? she asked herself with a shudder.

'The men will see him when they come back,' he said briefly. 'Assuming that we do not have to begin rounding up the horses again,' he added as a sarcastic after-thought, and Julia decided to keep quiet. In any case, she was still frightened, the sound of the thundering hooves still in her mind, Luc's violence still ringing in her ears and the marks of his fingers still burning into her shoulders.

The others were still not back but as the car came to the door, Rosanne appeared and at the sight of her Julia couldn't help stiffening even though she thought herself a fool. How could Rosanne have known that she would get herself into such a situation? After all, anyone with any sense would not have left the car, anyone with even one ounce of sense would have run for the car at the sound of the horses. It was just that she had not known what was happening and then had been almost hypnotised by the wild beauty, the unreality.

'Can you walk?' Luc helped her from the car and steadied her for a second.

'Yes, I'm all right, thank you. If you hadn't . . .'

'I have no desire to be reminded!' he said harshly, brushing aside the beginnings of her thanks before she could even start. 'You are soaking wet. You had better shower.'

'What is it?' Rosanne was right up to them, her voice sharp with interest.

'Nothing!' Luc's terse voice would have been enough to stop anyone but she still stood there, her hand coming to his arm, ignoring the angry signs.

'But Luc, what has she done? What happened?'

'Mind your own business!' Luc said rudely and sharply, startling Julia as much as Rosanne, and when she heard nothing else, she hurried to her room, to shower and change before anyone else could see her predicament.

She was not all right really. She knew that as she stood shivering under a hot shower. She was still frightened and shocked and the sight of Rosanne had brought it racing back. Common sense told her that it was all her own stupidity but she was not as a rule stupid. Things like this did not happen to her. She suddenly realised with great astonishment that she was crying quietly and she recognised delayed shock. It was ridiculous, pitiful!

'Julia!' Luc's voice in her room was the last straw and she felt wild with anger at him. He had no right simply to walk in like that.

'Julia!' Before she could even complete the switching off of the shower he was there, staring angrily at her.

'Luc! *Please!*' There wasn't a thing in reach that she could get to cover herself and he grunted angrily, tossing her a thick towel and turning away to her bedroom.

'Can't you even answer when I call to you?' he snapped. 'I imagined that you were collapsed in here!'

'Oh, get out! And close that door!' The tears were a mixture of anger, shock and shame now, but they rolled down her face and he slammed the door for good measure.

He was still in her room when she came out secure in a thick towelling robe. He was standing looking out of the window and she went for him before he had even the time to turn.

'You have no right to walk into my room like this! I'm not a little serving wench on your estate! Don't do it again!' She knew that there was an edge of hysteria in her voice but she was past caring. Everything went wrong with Luc. He *made* everything go wrong!

He turned slowly and looked at her a funny expression in his eyes.

'What are you so desperate about?' he said quietly. 'I was merely anxious about you.'

'You had no right simply to walk in there!' she stormed, making matters even worse.

He stared at her oddly, the dark eyes holding hers until her face flushed even more and then he ran his hand over his face almost wearily.

'Why do I get this feeling that I have every right?' he mused softly, his dark face sombre. 'Why do I feel that I have no need even to speak, that I can simply reach out for you?' He seemed to shake himself out of the peculiar mood and his eyes focused sharply on her startled face. Nobody had ever been able to silence her like Luc. She was stunned and puzzled.

'I want to know why you were there,' he said determinedly, back to normal with a vengeance. 'I want to know why you picked that exact spot at that exact time when we were doing the drive!'

'Obviously I didn't know, unless of course you think that I'm suicidal.' She turned away and began to brush her hair to escape those probing eyes, but he strode across and took the brush from her, slamming it on the dressing-table without more ado.

'You did not go there by chance! It is out of the way— difficult to find. There is not a person on the *manade* who does not know that today we were driving the horses in in readiness for the fair. So who told you to go there?'

'Is there a fair?' she said guilelessly, the soft word to turn away wrath, but he was not to be sidetracked.

'Julia!' he said dangerously. 'Stop this nonsense! Why were you there?'

'I was doing a sketch for a painting.' She looked away, but the hard hand came to her face, tilting it to the light.

'Why are you protecting Rosanne?' he said softly, his narrowed eyes on her face.

'You can't possibly know that.'

'Nobody else would do it,' he assured her. 'Justine adores you. Lucille admires you and she is, in any case, the gentlest of creatures. Maryse is your friend and

Philippe—well, he imagines that with a little encouragement he could fall in love with you. Who is left but Rosanne?'

'I'm sure that she didn't realise...' Julia said quietly, her head bowed as soon as he released her face.

He gave a grunt of exasperation and then to her astonishment he drew her forward and folded her in his arms, a hard wall of protection that seemed to enclose her tenderly.

'I cannot always be on hand at the correct time,' he murmured against her still wet cheeks. 'I want you to promise me that you will take care in the future. There is not a great deal of danger in this land but it is there for the seeking.' He tilted her face and looked at her intently. 'You will take care?'

'Yes,' she whispered, blissfully happy for this one moment, and a smile grew deep in his eyes as he cupped her nape with one warm hand.

'Then I will forgive you for being a nuisance and for probably costing me another day's work,' he assured her softly.

'I'm sorry,' she whispered, her eyes clinging to his.

'Maybe I am not,' he murmured quietly, his eyes searching her flushed face, and he suddenly pulled her closer. 'I did not come here to hold you,' he muttered against her hair, 'but now that I am here, it seems to be inevitable.'

It was. Inevitable was the only word that she could think of, too. In spite of her knowledge that this was so pointless she melted at his touch, her breathing instantly slow and uneven, and he drew back to search her entranced face, to look into her dazed eyes.

'Julia! *Pour l'amour de Dieu!*' he murmured, but his will was not strong enough for this any more than hers, and with a deep groan he held her tightly to him, his lips closing over hers, stifling her protests as his hands moulded her to the hardening planes of his body.

Only the loud bang of a door along the passage brought them back to reality and he put her away harshly.

'Truly, I am losing my mind!' he said bitterly.

'And so am I!' Julia cried, shaken by the depths of her feelings and hurt by his rejection. 'There's a great deal of truth in what they say about proximity. There must be, knowing as I do that...!'

'You know precisely nothing!' he rasped, turning to the door and opening it wide. 'We know more about each other since this afternoon than you will ever find out about me from anyone else, and what we know is the truth, not some wild fantasy!'

'You don't know anything about me,' she whispered, aware of the way that sound carried in this house.

'Wrong!' He stared at her with hard, dark eyes. 'I know that you are mine for the taking. Next time, perhaps I will take you!' He left angrily and Julia sank to the bed, utterly shaken.

Rosanne was not there at dinner time and Julia could only speculate that Luc had taken her to task for her actions. It made her feel guilty, because she could not really imagine that anyone would deliberately have done it. Even so, it was a relief not to have to face her and Luc, as usual, was back to normal, silent and dark, his conversation for Lucille when he bothered to speak at all. He did not even glance at Julia, and she began to wonder if the incident in her room was all her fevered imagination.

Justine told Julia the next day that they were going to the coast. She assumed that Justine meant the whole family and that the coast would be only a few miles away but she was wrong.

'*Oncle* Luc has to go to Cap d'Antibes. We have a property there, hotels along the coast, and it is quite a while since he was there because I was in England with you. I am allowed to go sometimes and we stay at one of our hotels. It is rather grand!' she finished with a smug little smile that brought an answering smile to Julia's face.

'Then I'm sure that you'll have a lovely time.'

'Ah! You are to come too, Julia!' Justine said gleefully. 'I shall be alone when *Oncle* Luc is working and, as you are here to take care of me, I expect that you will be coming along. I have not mentioned it to *Oncle* Luc but...'

'What have you not mentioned to *Oncle* Luc?'

He was there, his movements as silent and controlled as usual, and Julia found her face flushing although she tried to stay calm.

'I want Julia to go with us to Cap d'Antibes!' Justine said determinedly. She was not now anxious when Luc came upon them suddenly and Julia was sure that she was getting over her problems. Here, though, it seemed that she had one of her own. 'I would rather be with her than with any one of your lady friends when you are busy. They are very boring and Julia is fun. I'm sure that she will take me swimming instead of looking in the windows of dress shops!'

'Suddenly you are a very forward young lady,' Luc murmured with a mocking severity, clearly delighted at this return to normality. 'Is it possible that I spoil you, I wonder?'

'Oh, please, *Oncle* Luc!' Justine was instantly contrite but still able to use her feminine wiles. 'Take Julia, and I will not ask for anything else for—for—a long time!'

'Perhaps Julia does not wish to go with us,' Luc said softly with a sideways glance at Julia that brought a shiver to her skin.

There was no time to reply because Rosanne appeared and Julia had to revise her opinion about Luc's having remonstrated with her. She was bright and smiling, reaching to kiss Luc's cheek.

What time do we leave for Cap d'Antibes?' she asked cheerfully, ignoring everyone but Luc.

'We leave in the late afternoon, there was no need for you to arrive so early. Julia and Justine are coming but first there are Justine's morning lessons.'

Julia had already decided that she was not going but this now left her in the position of either a quiet scene with Justine or an open battle with Luc. His dark eyes seemed to acknowledge that fact with satisfaction.

'It is a very long drive. You had better pack things for two days and remember to travel in something light,' he said, looking directly at her. His dark eyes left hers to survey the molten sky. 'There is a gathering storm but maybe it will not hit us. Nevertheless, it is very sultry and the sea air will be good for you both.'

There was no getting out of it and, as they later gathered to leave, with Lucille to wave them off and

Maryse mournfully wishing that the bank would close its doors and set her free for a few days to go with them, Philippe appeared and slid into the back of the car with Julia and Justine.

'I didn't know you were coming!' Rosanne exclaimed sharply. She had placed herself in the front of the car with Luc, settling herself comfortably, and Julia was thankful that the big Mercedes estate car gave plenty of room to be well back. She did not want to hear Luc speaking to her.

'Naturally Philippe is coming,' Luc said quietly. 'He also runs the business. You may be going for the shopping but Philippe and I have to work.'

'Justine is going to sunbathe and Julia is going to simply look beautiful,' Philippe said teasingly, and Julia was surprised to find that this silenced Rosanne completely. There were many undercurrents that she could not understand, but her inclination at the moment was simply to leave them to it and look after Justine.

She looked up and saw Luc's dark eyes regarding her seriously through the rear-view mirror, and she glared at him even though her heart leapt into her throat as their eyes met. He merely raised one black brow and said nothing at all for the whole time that they travelled, even though the journey seemed interminable.

Justine was fast asleep when they arrived, and Luc nodded to the boy who appeared as if by magic to collect the luggage.

'Put it all in my suite for now. I will sort it out later,' he ordered, picking Justine up and walking forward. 'You may put the car away!'

He was the owner and no mistake, and Julia's eyes scanned the front of the hotel. It was massive and had an air of luxury about it that the inside merely confirmed. This was not the sort of hotel that scarred the Mediterranean coast, it was no quickly erected building for the package-holiday business. Only the rich would be able to afford to stay here and, by the look of the guests, they were here in plenty. She hurried after Luc, feeling very creased and dishevelled, but Rosanne lingered, quite used to this place, greeting the guests that they met in the foyer as old friends, arranging meetings for later. Clearly she was well known here and Luc's frequent companion.

She took over from Luc as soon as he had placed Justine on her bed.

'If you will get her into bed,' he suggested quietly, 'she will probably sleep until morning; if not, she can have a meal in her room.'

When Julia merely nodded and got on with the task of undressing the sleeping child, he watched her for a moment and then turned abruptly to leave.

'Your room is next door,' he commented harshly. 'It is already opened for you.'

He did not even wait for a reply but later, as she had left Justine and inspected her own rather splendid room, he tapped on the door and came in.

'When you are ready, I will take you down to dinner,' he said coolly, coming no further in than the doorway.

'Oh! I—I wondered if I could eat here in my own room,' Julia said with a small look of pleading. She had no fancy to sit with Rosanne and Luc even if Philippe was there, and she felt too tired to make any sort of effort. Maybe it was the threatening storm, or maybe it was that being close to Luc and seeing him every day was beginning to take too much out of her.

She dropped her eyes at his probing stare.

'I had not intended that Rosanne should accompany us!' he said flatly.

'It's no business of mine!' Julia got out quickly, keeping her head averted. 'I'm here to look after Justine and nothing more.' She gave a little laugh. 'You probably had no intention of bringing me either. Justine invited me!'

'She did not,' he assured her softly. 'I had every intention of bringing you. You are tight as a drum. You need to relax, to unwind. I had imagined that Philippe would do most of the work this time while I helped you to relax.'

She moved further away, shaken by this admission, the usual excitement beating high inside her.

'Shall I order my own meal here?' she asked quietly, quite desperate for him to leave and not at all surprised when he muttered angrily that she was quite at liberty to do so and walked out.

Her breakfast was served in her room the next morning without her lifting a finger to order it and it came to her mind that Luc had washed his hands of her and was about to allow her to eat here and stay indoors for the whole of the time if she chose. It annoyed her out of all proportion to the imagined crime and she met him head on as he came in later.

'I'm not so decadent that I need breakfast in bed, thank you!' she snapped before he had even said good morning.

'It is not so much decadence as a presumption of tiredness,' he said with a wry smile of amusement, coming to lean against the dressing-table as she stood in the middle of the floor in her dressing-gown. 'In any case, *mademoiselle*, I did not order it. No doubt the staff assumed that as you were with me you were of the same inclination as the ladies who normally stay here and refuse to move until they have been fed.'

'Well, I'm not!' Julia snapped, quite taken aback by his slightly indulgent amusement. 'You had better make it clear that I'm Justine's nurse and not one of your lady-loves!' Her tongue was quite out of control and she turned away heatedly at his suddenly gleaming look.

'That sounds a little like jealousy,' he murmured quietly.

'Well, it most certainly is not!' she snapped, but he was behind her instantly, his hands on her shoulders, pulling her back against him.

'But I want it to be, Julia!' he said deeply and urgently. 'I want you to be jealous. If things were as I want them to be there would be only you and I here!'

'Luc!' she began but he turned her into his arms, enfolding her tightly, his hands warm against her nape.

'No!' he said vehemently. 'Do not tell me to stop.'

She looked up at him helplessly, utterly vulnerable, and then, almost in a trance, she stood on tiptoe and kissed him. It had been meant to be a brief kiss, an answer to the plea in his voice, but his body tightened against her, lightning flared between them and with a low murmur deep in his throat he parted her questing lips and began to kiss her deeply.

She seemed to be filled with light, floating, whirling and falling as Luc caught her against him, the hard length of his body pressed to hers as the harshness of the kiss turned to honeyed sweetness that filled her with shivering delight.

'Julia! *Chérie!*' he murmured hotly against her skin, his hands stroking her closer.

She had known that any sweetness from Luc, any tenderness would be the end of her, and this was sweet beyond her wildest imaginings. Her arms tightened around his neck and she clung to him with a kind of desperation, wishing the whole world away to prolong this rapture.

'You are killing me!' he gasped. 'I want to make love to you *now*, to begin and never stop.'

Two bodies on fire, they clung together breathlessly, both utterly dazed as Justine burst into the room without so much as a knock.

'*Ça alors!*' she gasped, her face reddening and then beaming with delight. 'Oh, *c'est belle*! *Oncle* Luc is kissing you. I am so happy!'

Greatly flustered, Julia could have wished that Justine had a slightly quieter voice, and she drew away from Luc who even now seemed reluctant to let her go. It was as well, though, for at that moment the door opposite and just to the left opened as Rosanne came out dressed for a day's shopping, her eyes furious and her face red as she took in the scene.

'I will go back to my room and then you can carry on kissing Julia, *Oncle* Luc!' Justine said loudly, her bright eyes narrowed and suddenly spiteful as she saw Rosanne. There was an adult assessment of the situation on her face that shocked Julia, and Rosanne's steps faltered just once before she swept off along the corridor, ignoring them all.

'Justine!' Julia reprimanded sharply, but the child skipped out of the room, ignoring her call this time. '*Now* look!' Julia started, turning to Luc angrily, although she was the one who had initiated the kiss, but he was utterly indifferent himself to either the spite of his niece or the cold fury of Rosanne.

'I am looking,' he said softly, his eyes still bright with desire, 'and I am remembering how you felt in my arms, pressed close to me. I will remember when next you pretend that you are not burning with the same fire that burns me!'

He turned away but paused at the door, his eyes running over her possessively.

'I shall be busy for most of the day but I have arranged for you to take Justine to the boat of a friend of mine. I presume that you are a good swimmer?'

'Y-yes.' She nodded, swallowing hard when he continued to allow his gaze to roam at will over her trembling form.

'Then you can spend the day in relaxing, swimming and sunbathing. The hotel will make you a packed lunch, the boat has every luxury, and provided that you do not overdo the sunbathing you will be safe. At least you will be out of harm's way!'

She had a good idea of what he meant. She had seen Rosanne's face, but Julia could not imagine that she would swim out to them. She just nodded numbly and he left as silently as he had come. She was left deeply in thought. Luc knew that Rosanne had deliberately sent her to the area of the drive but still he had brought her here, even if he had not at first intended to. He had not remonstrated with her either. His desire to join the two properties must be very strong.

The 'boat' proved to be a launch of considerable size, one that Justine was obviously well used to because she raced ahead after one of Luc's men had dropped them off, finding her way to the cabins and selecting one for Julia where she could change in private.

They were anchored a little way down the coast where there was a surprising amount of tranquillity and solitude, and as they were quite a few yards from the shore the water was green and crystal clear.

'Oh! It is wonderful!' Justine cried with delight. 'I shall race you to change and then we will swim.' She was back to being herself, a very uncomplicated child, and Julia could almost feel that she had imagined the sharp look of spite that had crossed her face that morning.

She raced to change, scared that Justine would try the water before she was ready to supervise, but the little girl was waiting dutifully, and laughed at Julia's flustered appearance.

'I would have waited!' she said merrily. 'I dare not do otherwise. *Oncle* Luc has threatened me with very big punishments if I do anything to spoil the day for you. I am to be on my very best behaviour,' she added with a quick grin.

'You always are!' Julia said loyally and received a small and most unchildlike knowing look before Justine declared that she was about to get into the water.

It was a wonderful day and Julia kept her mind most firmly away from Luc and the incidents of the morning, but now and again, the memory of his arms, his lips, came rushing back, flooding her with feelings that she could not control. He had said that he only had to reach for her and she would go to him and she knew that he was right. She had proved that to herself this very day.

CHAPTER EIGHT

JUSTINE was given an early meal when they returned to the hotel and after a day in the sun and in the sea she was quite ready for bed. Julia then had no excuse and after getting ready, she found her way to Luc's suite. That was not at all difficult. It was on the same floor and clearly was permanently reserved, for a plate on the door stated simply Saint-Michaud. The marquis did not allow the rooms to be let and it took a deal of courage to knock on the door and enter when his deep voice called.

'*Entrez!*'

Rosanne was in the room, dressed for dinner, and she regarded Julia slowly and carefully, her eyes taking in the shine of her fair hair, the light dusting of freckles that make-up could not conceal, and the beginnings of a golden tan. Julia felt most unsophisticated in her simple white sleeveless dress. What had appeared to be very dressed up in her old home town was definitely not the height of fashion here, and Rosanne's face told her that quite clearly.

'I—I thought that . . . Am I to go to dinner with you?' she asked as Luc simply looked at her.

'You are!' He seemed to pull himself out of his trance and walked forwards to take her arm. 'Now that you are here we wait only for Philippe and then we will dine. We have been waiting for you.'

'Have we?' Rosanne's little laugh said his words were merely pointless courtesy. 'I thought that we were merely enjoying our time together.'

Luc ignored her and Julia was pleased when Philippe came into the room, smiling when he saw her.

'I will take Julia off your hands for the evening if you wish,' he said pleasantly to Luc, his eyes flirting with Julia, but to her surprise, Rosanne spoke out quickly, rejecting that idea.

'We are all together surely,' she insisted, her arm sliding into Philippe's. 'A foursome is much better I think!'

'I would not have imagined so,' Luc murmured for Julia's ears alone, but she was too busy sorting this out. At this moment it seemed that Rosanne was hedging her bets. If she did not get Luc then she would have Philippe. Her deep blue eyes slid to Philippe and for once the smiling face looked a little grim.

Rosanne chatted constantly at dinner and both Luc and Philippe seemed to expect it, both treating her with indulgence until Julia felt that she herself might as well not have been there. Her subtle snubbing of Julia seemed to go unnoticed and it would have been altogether too much except for the fact that Luc's dark eyes rarely left her and her heart was too busy racing to be hurt.

The next afternoon, he joined them on the boat, coming out to them without warning and tying the small fast craft he had used alongside before swinging himself to the deck. Justine raced to him as usual and was lifted high in two strong, brown arms.

'You cheated!' she cried excitedly. 'You said that you would not have time to join us!'

'Well, I have made time,' he countered. 'Besides, I have to make sure that our English princess does not get too much sun.'

'I have looked after her!' Justine declared with a great deal of self-importance, and Luc's eyes slid over Julia as she sat on the deck in her dark blue bikini, her slender legs already golden tanned, the brief covering merely making her femininity more pronounced.

'You have done well,' Luc said softly, his eyes holding Julia's. 'For the rest of the day I will stay and help you.'

He went to change and Justine was instantly in a frenzy of excitement.

'Let us hide!' she whispered hurriedly. 'I will go to one place and you to another. *Oncle* Luc will love it!'

Julia doubted that. He was not the sort of man she could imagine playing at hide-and-seek, but nothing would have made her stay there to face those dark and burning eyes. As Justine fled to the other side of the boat to crouch down, trying to still her giggles, Julia slid over the side of the boat and into the warm clear water. Time to get out when Justine had either been caught or given the idea up altogether.

In the event it was a mistake. She did not even know that Luc was in the water until he surfaced beside her, looking directly into her eyes, and then clasping her warmly by the waist to take them both beneath the surface. She barely had the time to divine his intentions and take a deep breath before they were sinking into the clear green water, Luc pulling her close and finding her mouth with passionate urgency.

'I could stay here all day and all night,' he said as they surfaced together breathing deeply, his hands stroking over the warmth of her back. 'I could float on the water and kiss every inch of you!'

'*Oncle* Luc!' Justine's voice carried clear as a bell to them and he grinned widely as he turned to face her. 'You have not played the game properly!'

'I play by my own rules, *ma belle*!' he called back. 'But we will come on board and take coffee.'

He swam to the boat and climbed aboard, lifting Julia to the deck, his hands still lingering on her, and she blushed at the fiery passion in his dark eyes, not knowing whether to be thankful that Justine was there or not. Truth to tell, she did not want to protect herself from Luc. She had long ago admitted her feelings for him and, as he had said, it was inevitable. Rosanne and the mystery of Justine's silence were far from her mind.

The long, hot afternoon drew slowly on and they moved into the shade of the bright canopy of the boat, where, after a while, Justine put her head on her arm and fell asleep. Instantly Julia was in a panic. Luc had changed to white shorts, his legs brown and bare, his broad chest shadowed by dark curling hair, but she was still in her bikini that had long since dried. She felt altogether too vulnerable.

'I think that we should be going back, don't you?' she said in a low voice, her eyes on Justine. 'Maybe she's had too much sun.'

'She is simply tired, as all children are after a day of excitement,' he said off-handedly. 'She will be all right there. In any case, she is as dark as I. Your fair skin is the only skin at risk from the sun.'

'Well—well, I'll go and change anyway,' Julia said quickly but he did not even open his eyes.

She had barely closed her cabin door before it opened again and Luc was standing looking at her, his jaw tight, his breathing uneven, and he walked slowly in, closing the door behind him, reaching out in the small cabin and running his hand over her skin, down her arm and back again, across the rapid rise and fall of flesh that marked the mounds of her breasts, cupping her slender waist and drawing her close to his hard body.

'I think that you are trying to kill me slowly,' he breathed against the silken skin of her neck, 'and you are succeeding very well.'

His lips were devastating her, making her tremble all over, and she murmured her protest softly, her hands limply trying to fend him off.

'Shh!' he whispered. 'Come to me, Julia, beautiful, tempting Julia!'

'Luc!' Her little gasp of protest was really an admission of defeat, the only signal he needed, and he drew her down to the narrow bed, pulling her close, his hands exploring the satin softness of her body, his lips whispering heated words she did not understand.

The tiny bra surrendered too to his skilled fingers and he looked with passion at the firm rose-tipped breasts, leaning forward to rub his mouth gently against each sensitive tip, bringing soft moans of delight to the back of her throat.

She arched towards him, desperate for more, and he took the tip in his mouth, almost cruel in his hunger, gasping aloud as he gripped her waist and lifted her towards him, his body forcing her into the softness of the bed.

She forgot everything except the moment, the burning need to be one with this dark, powerful man who filled her thoughts every waking moment and walked through her dreams.

'Luc!' Her hands clutched at his shoulders, feeling the taut muscles, the iron restraint, feeling too the moment when that stark control snapped and his mouth came down hard on hers, devouring her hungrily, his hands on her slender thighs, urging her against him. They were within seconds of being one and it was what she wanted.

'Julia! *Oncle* Luc!' Justine's voice, still clouded with sleep, called from the deck above and Luc rolled aside, coming to his feet, his breathing harsh and unsteady.

'Dieu!' he grated. 'When will I be able to live my own life?'

Her breath still rasping in her throat, Julia lay dazed, looking up at him, and he reach down to her, pulling her to her feet.

'Get changed!' he said tightly, his eyes still bright with hunger. 'You were quite right. It is time that we went back.'

She could only nod stupidly, unable still to feel shame that she was almost naked and that his eyes still devoured her. With Luc, it was right, everything that she wanted. Dazedly she tried to pull her mind to the present to battle with her own desire and she hurriedly donned her clothes, following him with as much speed as possible.

She found herself left pretty much to Philippe at dinner that night. Rosanne was with Luc, determinedly so, and Philippe's eyes followed them ruefully as they danced.

'She will get him,' he murmured almost to himself. 'We have always spoiled her and now she sees no reason to deny herself anything she wants.'

'You've always known Rosanne?' Julia asked quietly, her eyes on Luc as he smiled down at the girl.

'Since we were children,' he assured her. 'At least, since Rosanne and I were children. I cannot remember Luc ever being a child. I think sometimes that he never was.' He laughed a little harshly. 'We all followed Luc around. Even when Jules was there it was always Luc. He was the oldest, the steadiest, the strongest, the bravest. For a time she could not make up her mind which she wanted, Luc or me. It appears that she has now decided. Perhaps your coming has helped her to decide.'

'I'm sure that it hasn't,' Julia said softly. 'I've had no impact on any life other than Justine's!'

'And my mother's and Maryse's and mine,' he said with amusement, adding softly, 'and Luc's.'

'If—if he marries Rosanne, the property will be enormously enhanced.'

Philippe nodded, his eyes leaving the two who were dancing. He looked impatient with himself and turned his full attention on Julia.

'When my father died,' he explained, 'the property was divided as he felt—fairly. Luc was now the Marquis de Saint-Michaud and the lion's share went to him. Jules was next. The property that is now Luc's belonged to Jules. He and Deirdre lived there with Justine. I got a lesser share of things as I was only a son by his second marriage. Maryse got even less—she is a girl!' he grimaced. 'My father, you understand, was a very old-fashioned man. Luc was not pleased. Always he has worked the hardest, protected us, guided us. The Manade de Michaud was my mother's home, our home and clearly Luc would one day marry. What would he do? Throw us out? He was angry about it all.'

He was building a picture of past events that fascinated Julia. Her mind saw Luc as he had been before, understood his care for them all.

'When Jules died,' Philippe continued. 'Luc divided things again, to his own satisfaction. He took the other *manade*, leaving us our home whatever he decided to do. The lands around the Manade de Michaud are ours, Maryse's and mine when we are thirty. Luc's land stretches to the edge of the Dupin land and if he marries Rosanne, it will be a small kingdom for these parts. If he does not marry, Justine will inherit all of that, for Jules.'

'And more, if he marries Rosanne,' Julia murmured, her eyes drawn back to them.

'That is true,' Philippe assured her. 'The title should have land, undivided land more than he now possesses. He knows that, and the Dupins would not at all object to a title in the family. I do not, however, think it wise to guess what Luc will do. I have known him all my life, tried to keep up with his thoughts and actions, and still I cannot. Whatever he does it will certainly be for the good of the family, of this I am sure.'

'And if Rosanne chose you?' Julia asked quietly.

'I doubt if I could handle her,' Philippe said, his eyes narrowed on the pair of them. 'As I said, we have always spoiled her. She is amusing, wilful, very capable but a little unpredictable. I think that only Luc could handle

Rosanne.' He didn't sound as if he even wanted to try, and Julia's secret thoughts that he too loved the girl began to fade. She admitted that she did not understand any of them.

She was withdrawn when they came back to the table, and after a while Luc seemed to lose patience with her. She was not going to allow herself to be hurt again. He could already call her with a look, melt her with one touch and he had done. He was obviously contemplating marriage to Rosanne and she had had her fill of treachery with Graham.

Luc arrived before Justine next morning. He tapped lightly on the door and came into the room, his face so filled with delight at the sight of her that she could not bear to look at him. She turned her head away and when he advanced into the room, puzzled by her attitude, she glanced at him coldly.

'I had imagined, Monsieur Marchal, that this was my room!' she said with all that was left of her hospital manner. 'If you could tell me what you want then perhaps we can deal with it and you can go.'

'Julia?' There was no anger in his voice, merely astonishment. She knew that she had puzzled and even angered him last night by being withdrawn, but the last time they had been alone together she had been more than ready to belong to him and they both knew it. He walked forward and she sprang to her feet, everything about her defensive and angry.

'Don't make the mistake of touching me, *monsieur*!' she said sharply. 'If you do, I swear that I'll scream so loudly that the whole of the hotel will be alerted!'

The delight had died from his face and now the puzzled look was replaced by narrow-eyed anger.

'So, *mademoiselle*!' he grated harshly. 'Yesterday's game is over? Today I am to be starchily reminded of my duty to you and of your position in my life?'

'There was no game,' Julia said quietly, 'and my position is merely in Justine's life, and as to that...'

She got no further. He held up his hand imperiously.

'Do not trouble to continue!' he snapped. 'You wish to go home, back to England. Very well, I agree! You have tired of your time with us in the Camargue. You can no longer tolerate our ways. It is quite all right. I will arrange it. Justine will manage without you and so will I!'

He turned abruptly to leave but Julia was too hurt, too shocked to let it be left like that.

'The ways are stranger than I thought!' she cried bitterly. 'What were you doing yesterday on the boat, taking your frustrations out on me?'

He turned very slowly, his eyes cold and dark, a bleak harshness to his face that was frightening.

'And what does that little outburst mean, *mademoiselle*?' he asked coldly. 'You have invented another reason to distrust me?'

'I haven't invented anything,' Julia said quietly, turning away from his anger.

'Perhaps not!' he bit out. 'The thought of my alien life, my dark ways are quite enough to fill you with distrust without any invention. I know this already. You cannot comfortably accept us!'

'I accept Lucille and Maryse! I accept Philippe! I count them my friends! It is your behaviour I cannot accept. I love a man who...!'

She was stunned at her own outburst and the words she had chosen. She had been about to say that she loved a man who was going to marry someone else and that he was merely playing with her affections. Until the thought had come into her head and so nearly been blurted out she had not even realised the depths of her hurt and jealousy.

He stared at her as if she were a stranger, a stranger with a mind quite beyond his comprehension.

'You still love this man who has deserted you? You are quite prepared to go back and allow him to see you when his new wife is not there? Is this why you are so frequently anxious to go, to leave the Camargue? There is no need for evasion and subterfuge, *mademoiselle*! Do not bother! I will see that when we return you are on the next flight from Marseilles!'

He turned and strode to the door and reality swept over her. He had said that he wanted her to be jealous. She had been! She had not given him any time to speak, to explain. She had only Philippe's suppositions to base her ideas upon, those and her own knowledge of Rosanne. Would Luc kiss her, hold her, if he intended to marry another person?

'Luc!' She took a step towards him but stopped as the dark, cold eyes met hers with the same look he had given her when he had first seen her. What was she doing here? He had dismissed her from his mind, left her utterly.

'I preferred it when you called me *monsieur*, Mademoiselle Redford!' he said coldly, turning to walk from the room.

It was clear to Julia that he would never speak to her again and that in the morning he would book her flight to England. She was panic-stricken at the idea of leaving him and filled with shame when she realised the extent of her jealousy. He had been silent on the way back to the *manade* and she had no chance to speak to him alone until the others had gone to bed and Luc was securely in his study, the house silent around him.

She knocked on the door, shivering at the cold and harsh sound of his command to enter. He looked more cold than ever when he saw that it was Julia.

'Tomorrow, *mademoiselle*!' he said abruptly, turning back to the papers on his desk. 'Your flight will be booked at first light, never fear!'

'That's not why I came,' Julia got out before her nerve deserted her altogether.

'Then why?' he asked harshly, his dark head lifting as he regarded her from beneath black brows.

'I came to tell you that I'm sorry. I had no right to—to be so harsh, to judge you so unjustly. I—I don't fit in here—don't understand. It's like another world. I'm here to nurse Justine and not to criticise you.'

'You should!' he said decisively. 'I have no right to make love to you. You have a career of your own, a home of your own that is totally unlike this.' He stood and went to look out of the window at the still night, the rising moon. 'Oh, what is the use? You will never understand us. You are not Camarguais!'

'No, I'm not!' Julia said desperately, afraid to speak in more than a whisper, feeling that her very life hung by a thread.

'It will not be necessary to understand when you are back in England and many miles away from this place!' he said bitterly, still turned away from her.

It was now or never. Every instinct told her that and she hedged up the remains of her courage.

'Don't send me back, Luc!' she pleaded softly. 'Please don't send me away!'

'Why should you wish to stay when your opinion of me is so low, so deeply distrustful?'

He spun round and faced her but her courage was not that strong. She wanted to say, 'Because I love you,' but the words would have taken more strength than she possessed.

'*Please*, Luc!' she whispered, her eyes downcast, and he muttered under his breath, mocking the words.

'*Please*, Luc! You say it many times, but never for the right reasons!'

'You wanted me to stay with Justine and I want to!' she said firmly, taking a grip on her mind. 'Now you want me to go. Has Justine suddenly become unimportant? Has this sunk to the level of a personal battle?'

'You are interested enough in me to battle, Julia?' he asked, his eyes dark and probing.

'I came to do something and I haven't finished it yet,' she said quietly, her hands clenched to stop the trembling.

'The serious and determined Sister Redford. You are then nothing more than a perfectionist? Very well,' he finished sombrely. 'We will try again. I suppose that Justine has become too much part of your life for you to leave her willingly, but do not forget that you have a life of your own. It was you who said that this was merely a temporary arrangement.'

He turned away, not seeing the look on her face. Her reasons for coming here in the first place were now utterly forgotten. It was Luc who was too much a part of her life, Luc whom she could not leave! Clearly, though, the interview was over, and once again Luc was dark, unfathomable and unreachable.

She whispered goodnight and went to bed, and as far as she knew he did not even answer.

The next afternoon, though, when Julia was sitting in the garden, Luc came to find her. She had not felt like venturing out after the trauma of the previous day, and as for Rosanne, there had been no sign of her. The whole trip to the coast had left Julia feeling listless and unsure and she looked up at Luc with some misgivings as he hovered over her.

'There is no need to brace yourself for attack,' he remarked drily as she regarded him wide-eyed. 'Get your bag, I am taking you into town. You will have a chaperon, never fear!' he added with a sardonic look at her flushed face. 'Justine is also invited.'

Justine appeared at that moment wreathed in smiles and dancing forward, apparently filled with glee.

'We are going to inspect the arena! The *bull* ring!' she added at Julia's mystified expression. 'Also the gypsies have arrived and *Grand-mère* Lucille is there already! Hurry, Julia! It is an exciting day! Tomorrow they will run the bulls and *Oncle* Luc will be the best of all!'

Julia was sure that whatever he was to do he would be the best at it but his greatly amused expression kept

her silent and there was a light-hearted air about him
that took her breath away. Inexplicably, unbelievably,
he had forgiven her! She needed no further bidding and
Luc set off to the town with two very excited people
beside him.

The place was thronging with visitors, the atmosphere
totally changed. Suddenly, it had become a holiday resort
and Luc, rather than frowning on this change, seemed
to enjoy it. There were tourists in shorts and sun-dresses
in the main square and here and there the vivid clothes
of the newly arrived gypsies.

'I see *Grand-mère*!' Justine was out of the car as fast
as a little cat, but Luc caught her as she passed and swept
her up to his shoulder.

'Not so fast, *ma belle*!' he said amusedly. 'If you wish
to desert us for your grandmother then we will hand you
over properly. I do not wish to find that you have disappeared into some caravan, never to be seen again.'

'They love me!' Justine protested, wriggling uselessly.
'Almost, I am one of their own!'

'But not quite!' Luc remained her.

'Maryse is! And also Philippe!' she said with a great
deal of pride.

'That much is true,' Luc agreed quietly with a sidelong
look at Julia's face. The whole thing was beginning to
dawn on her, and when she found herself surrounded
by dark-skinned laughing people and heard Lucille
answering their questions in the Romany tongue, everything fell into place. The amused, knowing eyes, the dif-
ferently textured skin, the diffidence of the woman who
had after all married Luc's father and for a time at least
had been the wife of the once Marquis de Saint-Michaud.

Lucille was with her people and happy as Julia had never seen her before.

They were a handsome people, proudly unaware of the interests of the tourists, and by the way they were greeted it was clear that there was a special affection for them here in the Camargue.

'You think that tomorrow will be a bright day, Monsieur le Marquis?' one grinning old man asked Luc.

'You tell me, Denys!' Luc laughed, handing the wriggling Justine over to Lucille and the admiring gypsy woman. 'It is your business to know these things.'

'Storm clouds are coming!' the old man said, suddenly sombre, and for a second his sharp old eyes rested on Julia, giving her a weird feeling that was half premonition. 'For the *abrivado*, though, we will have sunshine, great heat and plenty of dust.'

'I can believe it!' Luc said with a laugh. 'And plenty will taste the dust in their mouths tomorrow!'

He had a quick word with Lucille and then led Julia away, making for the shops at the side of the road.

'Before we inspect the arena we will get you a hat to cover that bright head and protect that haughty nose!' he said drily, his hand firmly and warm on her arm.

'There is nothing haughty about my nose!' Julia retorted still rather dazed by the latest revelations, bemused by Luc's ready forgiveness.

'Not even when you now know that my stepmother is a gypsy?' he countered wryly. 'Your great friend Maryse and your great admirer Philippe have true Romany blood running in their veins.'

'You expect me to be shocked?' Julia stopped in the road and looked at him. 'Lucille is gentle, kind, a very handsome woman and there is nothing wrong with Maryse and Philippe either. Why, in England, Philippe would certainly turn any girl's head!'

'But not yours, *mademoiselle*?' he enquired softly.

She didn't answer. He already knew that he only had to look at her to turn her to shivering delight. He began to laugh softly, leading her into the nearby shop and buying the floppy hat that he had promised a few days before.

'*C'est élégant!*' he pronounced, standing back to look at her. 'It hides a little of the beauty perhaps but then again, it protects the bright head and the haughty nose!'

The woman in the shop was delighted with this banter but Julia was quite flustered. This was Luc as she had never seen him before and she hardly dared to breathe in case he withdrew and left her alone and unhappy.

The arena was starkly splendid. It had once housed gladiators who fought to the death but now, with its arches still intact, its grand entrance restored, it held the bulls after the race through the town, the *abrivado*. Luc sat her in the seats half-way up where she could see all around, explaining that there was no intention to fight the bulls, only to take from their heads a small rosette strung between the horns.

'Naturally, the bull objects!' he said with a grin. 'The degree of his objection is the thing that brings the excitement and the challenge.'

'Do the horses get hurt?' Julia asked worriedly, thinking of the beauty of the wild white horses that she now took almost for granted.

'There are no horses, *mademoiselle*!' he said in a mockingly shocked voice. 'He who challenges the bull does so on foot and at his own risk. The horses are merely used in the *abrivado* and in the grand race that follows the robbing of the bulls!'

'Don't—don't people get tossed?' Julia asked.

'Frequently!' he agreed with a certain amount of relish that had her looking at him in horror. 'They are rarely badly hurt though. You will see many acts of courage tomorrow and quite a few of sheer stupidity but it is the *abrivado*, and then at night, there is the great fair and the dancing.' He looked at her steadily. 'You will not try to back out of it I hope? Your English nerves will be up to it?'

'If yours are!' she said pertly and he laughed, that low laugh that she heard so rarely.

'Oh, I have nerve for almost anything, English princess!'

After he had looked the ring over and talked to the men working there, they went back out into the sunny streets, and though there was still that slight air of aloofness about him, Julia knew that for the moment he was as relaxed as she was ever likely to see him, and in some way that she did not understand, he was happy. It was all she could wish for.

They were almost ready to leave and were looking for Justine when she saw Graham. At first, she could not believe her eyes and she drew close to Luc's side, trying to hide as much as she could, thankful that the hat hid her bright head and made her less obvious in the crowds who were mostly dark-haired and French, or gypsies. It was Graham, though. She had the chance to take a good look at him and she spent the rest of the time with her heart in her mouth, her tense state at first mystifying and then annoying Luc.

'You are perfectly safe in a crowd!' he said with some asperity. 'And I promise that I will have you back at the ranch before it is time for dinner. If you wish, I will get one of the gypsy boys to escort you, perhaps you will feel safer with one of them. I know your opinion of me!'

'I feel perfectly safe with you!' she said rapidly, trying to plead with him, but he was not at all pleased.

'What is wrong with you?' he demanded. 'For the last half-hour you have been like a frightened child. What have I done now to upset you?'

'It's nothing. *Please*, Luc!'

'*Please*, Luc!' he mocked. 'How many times have I heard that already?'

His light-hearted mood had gone and there was nothing that she could do to bring it back. The drive back to the *manade* was not the joyous thing that the outward ride had been and Julia spent all evening on edge, waiting for the telephone to ring, or for Graham simply to arrive. It was too much of a coincidence that he should have turned up here, and she could only think that Jean Todd had somehow been persuaded into giving up her new address. She wished that she had never written to her.

CHAPTER NINE

IN THE morning, though, her mind had pushed Graham away, right into the background. He had never been in touch and maybe he was merely a tourist, passing through. Maybe he was on his honeymoon, she thought with a grimace. It was strange that the idea of being married to Graham, an idea she had once accepted so readily, now gave her an attack of shudders. Luc was the only one who would ever be right for her, she knew that. Only Luc's arms could satisfy and thrill her.

The men had all gone on ahead and Julia found herself driving Justine, Lucille and Maryse in the small car that Luc had given her. The whole town seemed to be full of noise, bright colour and music. It was a holiday and everyone was out, the young gypsy guitarists strolling along, playing and dancing as they went, flashing their dark eyes at the girls and adding to the excitement.

There were stalls, horse traders, everything beribboned and bright, and the atmosphere was electric with expectancy. The tourists on the terraces of the cafés, sipping their coffee and watching the passers-by, the roguish-looking gypsies, the citizens on holiday for the day, all of them were out, all waiting for the event that marked this day, the *abrivado*.

Suddenly a great shout went up.

'They're coming!'

There was a rush to get to the sides of the street, everyone jostling for a good view, and Julia caught her breath in excitement, her hand tightening on Justine's as the black bulls came charging down the wide avenue.

Behind them and flanking them were the *gardians* riding the fast white horses of the Camargue. They were grim-looking, determined, and the pace was furiously fast.

'They must get the bulls to the arena without losing any!' Lucille said excitedly.

'The boys will try to stop them! It is a great game!' Justine shouted, jumping up and down.

It seemed to Julia that it was an insane game to try to stop this wild charge. She saw Luc and Philippe at opposite ends of the crescent of riders and it all seemed so grim, so deadly serious. But the crowd joined in with gusto doing all in their power to stop the racing bulls. They threw flour-bombs, sticks and even fireworks, and finally to Julia's horror three young man threw themselves under the flashing hooves to capture a bull.

As the riders thundered past she saw that they had succeeded in detaining it. Once had its horns, another its tail, and the third was half-way on to its back. The triumph was short-lived however because almost instantly the enraged animal was free and the crowd scattered to run for their lives as it charged everywhere, seeking revenge.

It was Luc who came back for it. Trident in hand, his hat pulled well down against the dust, he nodded in acknowledgement to the breathless youths who had performed the impossible, his smile a flash of brilliantly white teeth against his dark face before he skilfully used his horse, sidestepping around the bull, his voice calming, the trident warning. It trotted away, the crowd once more merry as he left. They had in no way impeded the capture. The game was over.

'Ciel!' Lucille mopped her face as they stepped off the terrace where they had sought shelter. 'It was a great *abrivado*! But it took three to get the one bull. This year, the bulls are stronger than ever, Luc told me this morning. Let us hurry to the ring and take our places!'

Julia was still reeling from it all, astonished at the great relish with which this quiet and self-effacing woman had cheered the feats of madness. There was more to come, but she was drawn into the life of the Camargue and into Luc's life. She suddenly found herself laughing, Justine's hand in hers, her arm tucked into Lucille's as they hurried to see the bulls take their revenge.

'What of that, English girl?'

The others were all there in reserved seats and Philippe challenged her as she came along the row with Justine and Lucille.

'Madness!' she said with a wide grin that apparently pleased him.

Luc said nothing. Rosanne was at his left side and she did not even raise her eyes, but Luc's eyes held Julia's and he patted the seat beside him.

'Sit here!' he ordered quietly and she had no alternative but to obey, although she saw Rosanne stiffen and glance across with cold eyes. Maryse looked on with startled gaze and then carefully looked away, her lips edged with a pleasant smile.

The bulls were now the masters. Each bull was called out by name and challenged by a group of young men dressed in white. They raced around the dusty arena dodging the razor-sharp horns, reaching for the rosette and darting away with or without it as the bull guarded his treasure and attempted to maim them.

They were swift-footed and they had to be! Many were reduced to leaping the barriers and leaving the ring entirely, an enraged bull close behind, but many succeeded in their goal. Any bull who kept his rosette for fifteen minutes was the winner and retired from the ring to the cheers of the crowd.

But the greatest was Tamerline, a bull from Luc's own ranch.

'He is the very devil!' Philippe remarked to Luc. 'Nobody will win against him, and they will be lucky not be tossed badly!'

And they tried, two of them finding themselves high in the air and landing well behind the barriers, lucky to have escaped so lightly. Nobody succeeded. It was all wildly exciting and as the danger seemed merely to bring on further acts of madness, Julia stopped worrying and joined in with the rest, cheering the bulls.

'That is the end!' Justine said confidently as the last bull was cheered from the ring, but there was an air of expectancy that kept the crowd in their seats and once again the loudspeakers blared.

'A challenge!'

The gates opened and Tamerline trotted back into the ring, his head high, his nostrils flaring, more annoyed than ever, the supreme champion, and as he circled the ring the crowd began to chant, 'Saint-Michaud! Saint-Michaud!', the cries growing to a great climax.

'*Mon Dieu!* You will not accept?' Philippe muttered, his hand on Luc's arm as he leaned across. 'He is a killer, that one, you know it!'

'I reared him, I am expected to take the rosette!' Luc said firmly, and to Julia's horror he stood and bowed to the crowd, walking then to the arena to the cheers which only maddened the bull further.

If she had been able to hold him back, she would have done. One look at the faces of his family was enough to tell her that this was not usual. The bull had been once in the ring and emerged victor. He was clever and angry, knowing now exactly what to expect, and she could see the great head turn, the glittering horns toss experimentally as the crowd hushed and Luc vaulted into the ring.

It was a lesson in nerve, in sheer skill, and in spite of her fear, Julia found herself watching with breathless admiration. The man and the bull circled each other, the animal seeming to realise that here was someone entirely different. And Luc moved like a great cat, making no attempt to take the rosette, his actions turning the bull this way and that, forcing him into the sort of footwork that she had seen him force from the horse as he had ridden back down the avenue to recapture the bull in the *abrivado*.

He seemed to be mesmerising it, taming it, holding it with his glittering eyes and with the lithe movements of his body. Then suddenly, like a bullfighter, he stopped, raised his hand and snapped his fingers, and before the bull could make a move, the rosette was snatched, safely in Luc's hand, and he strode to the barrier, vaulting to safety as the animal seemed to come out of some trance and charged madly but belatedly.

Luc was grinning widely and the crowd went mad, cheering and throwing their hats in the air, amused and delighted at this piece of sheer effrontery.

'Fantastique!' Philippe shouted, on his feet, cheering with the rest of them. 'He is the best! When he dies there will be a mighty *ramadan* as every bull mourns him as one of their own!'

'But not yet!' Luc retorted, gaining his seat and catching the tail end of Philippe's remarks. 'For now I am in one piece. And what of that, English girl?' he added, turning to Julia with a sardonic look, repeating the words that Philippe had said earlier.

'It was mad, dangerous and magnificent,' she said quietly, knowing well that her heart was in her eyes.

'Then for those words you shall become a queen instead of a princess for this day,' he said softly as he slid the rosette over her wrist, presenting it to her in front of everyone.

'He has claimed you for the dance!' Justine shouted loudly, clapping her hands gleefully. 'And you cannot refuse!' she added with even greater glee. 'It would be an insult, would it not, Philippe?'

'A rare insult indeed, as he has never bothered to do it before!' Philippe remarked, his eyes wide with speculation on Luc's dark face and Julia's rosy cheeks.

'Then I shall not refuse!' Julia said quietly, gathering her dignity around her quickly. 'I shall bear it with fortitude!'

There was a great laugh in which Luc joined, but Rosanne most certainly did not. She looked furiously at Julia and her hand tightened on Luc's arm with all the possessiveness of someone quite used to getting everything she wanted.

After that there was the great race around the streets when the *gardians* vied with each other to be first past the winning-post and gain the silver cup to be held for the year. Then, as the dusk of the Camargue crept stealthily into the brightly lit streets, the party from the Manade de Michaud went to the hotel to change for the dance. Justine was packed off to bed and a contented Lucille, who declared herself too exhausted to stay up any more, volunteered to sit with her.

The excitement still hung in the air as later Julia went with Maryse to join the others and make her way to the square, now bright with lanterns, where the dance was to be held. The night was softly warm and the blue silk dress whispered around her legs as she walked along beside Maryse.

As usual, Rosanne was there first and Julia had to admit that she looked very beautiful. She was clinging to Luc's arm as if to let go would be the end of her, and Julia wished that the incident at the arena had never happened. Much as she wanted to be in Luc's arms, she dreaded any scene that it might bring. It reminded her too of his intentions, which now, in the soft darkness, seemed real again. It was expected that he would be here with Rosanne. A marriage between them had probably been expected for years.

The men were in shirts and slacks, Philippe joining them, and when one of the young *gardians* came forward to claim Maryse for the dance Luc gave no sign of annoyance. Apparently a *gardian* could be trusted whereas the gentleman at the bank could not. She never doubted that Luc knew exactly what he was doing.

He suddenly turned to her, quietly disengaging himself from Rosanne and bowing over her hand in his usual sardonic way.

'For the evening you are claimed,' he said determinedly, 'and the dance begins. For this night, *mademoiselle*, you are *mine*!'

She had intended to refuse, her jealousy again at the very surface at the sight of him with Rosanne, but his eyes held hers hypnotically and she could do nothing but look back at him.

'You never meant it, surely, Luc?' Rosanne said with a hard little laugh.

'But I did,' he said softly, his hand held out. 'Julia knows that I did.'

For a moment his eyes were sardonic and she knew without doubt that he was thinking of his own words, 'If I reach for you you will come to me.' She looked back at him and placed her hand in his.

'You will have to make do with me!' Philippe said to Rosanne with what seemed to be a great deal of satisfaction but Julia did not look for the girl's reaction. Luc pulled her forward, right into his arms, smiling down at her as they began to dance, and as usual she let her heart over-ride her head.

It was easy to forget everything and it was all that Julia wanted to do. She realised that she was almost light-headed, prepared to live this night as if it were her last on earth. She saw nothing but the dark head bent to hers, felt nothing but the strong arms that held her ever closer. Sometimes they were in the glow of the lanterns, sometimes in the shadows at the side of the square, but Luc never relinquished her. Partners were changed and refound, laughter echoed above the music, but all the time the two of them seemed to be in a world of their own.

When the music finally stopped for a break she felt dazed and cheated, her bewilderment at first mirrored on Luc's dark face as he looked down at her before smiling in self-derision and leading her to the side of the square.

'I will get drinks for us,' he said softly. 'Stay exactly where you are. In this crowd it would take me some time to find you.'

It was an unnecessary worry. There was no way that anyone could part her from Luc while he wanted her. Her eyes followed him as he strode, dark and lithe, across the square. She could watch him all day and never tire of it. There was something in the air, something extra between Luc and herself. Excitement welled up inside her.

'Julia!' The hand that took her arm was not Luc's and for a second she gaped stupidly. 'My God! I've been trying to get to you all day! I saw you at the bull ring but you never looked across and I was too late to get to you when you left. If you hadn't been here tonight I don't think I would have ever been able to find you!'

It was Graham! For a second she just stared at him. He was like someone out of the very distant past, almost unrecognisable, nothing to do with her at all. She had completely forgotten about seeing him the day before and her fingers fretfully removed his hand without any conscious knowledge of having done it.

'What are you doing here? What do you want?'

She looked at him in near horror, thankful that the lights here were very low. In the break for the small band, the square echoed to the sound of flamenco music and the rhythmical chatter of castanets as the gypsies danced.

'Come over here, out of all this damned noise!'

Graham pulled her out of the square into the greater darkness of the street and she suddenly came to life.

'What are you doing here? I don't want to see you!'

Luc had told her to stay where she was and now Graham had moved her. She struggled, looking round for him, and to her astonishment, Graham shook her, his face angry and mean.

'Come to your senses, Julia!' he snapped angrily. 'I've been looking for you for two days, wandering about this town. I knew it was useless coming out to that ranch place. You've got yourself into a fix, haven't you, coming out here with that man, taking a job as a nursemaid!'

'Let me go!' Julia struggled wildly, but he pulled her into his arms, more than a little wild himself.

'I've come for you, Julia!' he said determinedly. 'It was all a mistake. Gloria wasn't like you, nobody is. I've told her I still love you. We belong together, Julia, we always did!'

'We don't! I'm not coming back! I don't want to be with you!'

'I know you do! I'll not let you ruin our lives!'

To her horror, he bent his head to kiss her, grasping her cruelly in his frustration, his lips hot and violent, his strength forcing her head back against his arm. Sheer panic shot through her; not that she was afraid of Graham in this town where there were people so close, but the idea of other lips than Luc's on hers was distasteful to the point of revulsion.

She was powerless to move and when he raised his head triumphantly, utterly careless of whether he had hurt her or not, she opened her eyes to see Luc standing a few feet away, two glasses in his hands, his face tight and cold. She just looked at him, seeing it all from his point of view, unable to utter a word in her own defence.

He simply opened his fingers and allowed the glasses to drop to the floor, ignoring the sharp splintering sound as they smashed on the cobbles of the darkened road, and then he strode forward with murder in his eyes.

Graham never knew what happened. Savagely pleased with himself at his ability to subdue Julia, he was suddenly spun round and Luc's fist crashed into his jaw, all the power and fury of the superbly fit body behind it. Graham went down silently and Luc turned on his heel, leaving the square without a backward glance.

'*Mon Dieu!* What is it? What has happened?'

Philippe was suddenly there, his arm coming around Julia who still stood dazed, and all she could do was shake her head stupidly.

'Who is this man?' Philippe asked urgently. 'It is unlike Luc to attack anyone without good cause.'

'I knew him in England,' Julia got out dazedly, 'and Luc thought . . . he thought that . . . !'

'Go after him!' Philippe said quickly. 'Explain!'

'How can I?' Julia asked miserably. 'He's so angry and he's never going to believe me.'

'He is not if you never explain!' Philippe exclaimed with exasperated logic. 'He singled you out for the dance. Now he has been forced into this! Can you not see what it all means to him? He is a proud man and I know him. Explain now or you will never again get the chance to do so!'

'He'll never believe . . . !'

'Then you had better see to it that he does! I will take care of this odd-looking person,' he added as Graham began to move with a groan.

Julia took one disgusted look at Graham and then ran. She had a very good idea where Luc would be going. He would be heading to his own place, away from everyone, and she was not at all sure that she could find her way there, especially in the dark.

Luc, it seemed, though, had not parked as conveniently as she had and as she ran from the square, she saw him turn out of a side street into the main road. The Land Rover was not yet going fast, and she stood where he could see her, determinedly blocking his way.

He stopped but clearly had no intention of speaking even when Julia came to the open window and stood looking at his tight face.

'Luc! Why did you just take off like that?'

The run had made her breathless and she leaned against the dusty Land Rover, wondering if he would simply drive off and knock her to the ground.

'I should have waited until you had had enough kisses from your fiancé?' he rasped savagely, not turning. 'Was my turn coming then, *mademoiselle*?'

Sarcasm was the last thing she wanted now and it infuriated her.

'Graham Adams is *not* my fiancé! He has not been my fiancé for some considerable time, as you well know!' she protested angrily.

'So I understood!' he snapped, turning to glare at her through narrowed eyes. 'When I find however that you have been writing to him, inviting him here to the Camargue, arranging to meet him, I begin to doubt my own beliefs!'

'I did *not* invite him here! You're no more surprised than I am. He must have got my address from Jean Todd, the sister at the hospital. He—he just—pounced on me.'

'And you were more than willing,' he said in disgust, turning away and restarting the engine.

'I wasn't! I wasn't willing at all! He hurt me, but then I don't suppose you think that it matters all that much,' Julia said quietly, all her temper dying away in misery at the realisation that his action had been only male pride, damaged ego. 'I'm not of the Camargue, as you said more than once. I can get myself in and out of my own troubles. All you care about is that the Marquis de Saint-Michaud may have been seen to be insulted. Your code of honour is very strange, *monsieur*. In England I would have expected to be rescued, not blamed.'

She turned away, giving up any idea of a plea to him. She wanted only to get away, anywhere rather than face his angry look, those tight and unforgiving shoulders. What had she done after all that needed forgiveness, except to love him when she had no right? Her eyes filled with tears. What was she doing here, racing after Luc? He wanted her but there was Rosanne, he had never denied it. The title and the land were deep in his blood and she was not of the Camargue, he had told her that more than once. Tomorrow she would go back home, to her father.

He accelerated away without a backward glance and she admitted that it was the end of her time here. She would explain to Justine. It was a long time now since she had felt any real concern about Justine's problems. As far as she could tell, Justine was well restored to her family. It was time she went back to hers.

Philippe seemed to have alerted the rest of the family and as she returned he was ushering them into the cars, his eyes flashing to her face and seeing the despair she could not hide.

'I will drive you home,' he said quietly. 'Maryse will take your car. Do not worry too much, Julia. Tomorrow Luc will see that this is all very unfair. He has the temper of a bull but it does not last.'

Tomorrow she would be gone. Julia simply nodded and sat in weary silence for the duration of the drive. Justine was still sleeping, and at the *manade*, Philippe carried her out and placed her in her own bed. Julia watched from the door, knowing that tomorrow she would have to harden her heart against any tears as she told Justine of her decision.

Already a red dawn was breaking over the Camargue and Julia knew that for herself there would be no sleep. Quietly she packed her things and then lay down for a few hours' rest, Luc's angry face in her mind. She could see nothing but darkness before her. She was hurt again. Her ways would always invite it. When she gave love it was always too deeply given, but this time she knew that there would never be another love. It had ended with Luc.

She was up at seven, breakfasting with the family, her explanations made. They were bewildered by her sudden decision to leave, only Philippe knowing why she must go home with such urgency.

'Whatever you have done, Luc will forgive!' Maryse said tearfully. 'Often he is angry but he is never unjust.'

'I do not think that Julia needs forgiveness,' Philippe said quietly. 'She has done nothing but give since she has been here, and she has given her gentleness and her kindness to all of us. It is private, Maryse, and should be left alone.'

He sounded like Luc and Julia was grateful to him. She went upstairs to Justine, who was awake but still not up. It had to be faced and she might as well do it now.

'How can you leave us?' Justine wept when Julia had explained that she must go back to England. 'I cannot manage without you, and what will *Oncle* Luc do? He also cannot manage without you!'

'I must go back to my own work,' Julia told her softly. 'My father needs me too. You're quite better now, darling. Don't forget that my father misses me. I was only here for a while. You always knew that.'

'What will I do though if *Oncle* Luc finds out that I know?' Justine wept. 'I cannot face him when he knows it was all my fault that they died.'

'Nothing was your fault!' Julia said firmly. 'Your father was driving the car. It was an accident.'

'It was not!' Justine stated wildly, her voice raised. 'Maman pulled the wheel. She tried to take the car from him. He was shocked and angry when she told him that *Oncle* Luc was really my father! What shall I do when *Oncle* Luc finds out that I know?'

For a second Julia was stunned into silence. All the looks that Justine had given Luc at first came back into her mind, the anxiety on her face until he spoke, and she knew that her secret was still safe, the unconscious decision to hide in silence when there was nowhere else to hide.

'Listen to me, Justine!' she said sharply, taking her small thin shoulders in her hands and forcing Justine to look into her eyes. 'You heard a quarrel, a grown-up quarrel. Grown-ups become angry and say things to hurt each other that they don't mean at all. If your mother said that then it was only said to hurt because she was angry. It is not true!'

'But you did not know them! How can you say it is not true?' Justine begged.

'I didn't know them, but I know your Uncle Luc,' Julia said quietly. 'It can't be true because he is a wonderful, honourable man, and even more than that, he loved your father as he loves you. You must never hurt him by telling him things that are not true.'

Justine nodded silently, the tension beginning to ease from her small shoulders.

'He will be hurt when you go,' she said, her dark eyes intent on Julia's face.

'No. He has you. He has his family and Rosanne and his land. You are all Camarguais. I am English and I need my own home and my own people. One day, darling, I'll come back to see you. Perhaps one day Uncle Luc will let you come to stay with me.' She kissed the thin, tear-wet face. 'You can make everyone happy, see that you do. We all have that duty.'

Julia walked quickly to the door, getting out before her resolve deserted her and almost stumbling into Lucille who was just outside.

'It is not true, Julia!' she said urgently. 'Justine is Jules' child. Deirdre was always cold, hurtful. We tried to tell Jules before the wedding but she was beautiful and determined. Only Luc would have been a match for such a one as she. She had no love for Justine, not even from the first, and I doubt if she ever loved anyone in her whole life. Whatever she said that night, it was not true! Luc kept well away from her. He disliked her always and showed it more often than not!'

'You don't have to tell me this, Lucille,' Julia said softly. 'I know it couldn't be true. Luc is a very special person and he could never do anything to hurt one of you. Now that Justine has said it, though, I think she'll simply forget it all after a while. So you see, I can safely go home and leave her to you.'

'I will drive you to Marseilles!' Philippe said sombrely as she went down to collect her suitcases from the hall. 'I do not see why this should be, but as you are determined on it, I will take you to the airport.'

They were silent on the journey, Julia sitting like a statue, icily cold in the hot sunshine, Luc's face before her as if he were there.

There was a flare of colour that caught her eyes and the flamingoes swept into the air, flame-bright against the blue of the sky. The tears came then, her icy restraint dropping away as she watched.

'Goodbye!' she whispered to herself, and she was not saying goodbye to the beauty of the birds alone. It was a cry from her heart to this land, this strange land that she would never see again, a final goodbye to Luc.

Once at the airport she was torn between a desire to leave at once, to get back to her father and grieve in silence for Luc, and a desire to stay, to turn back and seek him out. Philippe was grimly silent, his hand on her arm protective, none of the flirtatious humour about him now. He knew how she was feeling, she didn't doubt that for a moment.

She turned to him to say goodbye but their eyes met in startled glance as her name came over the loudspeakers.

'Will Sister Julia Redford please come to the telephone.'

It had to be repeated before either of them came to life and Philippe was more calm than Julia.

'It can be nothing serious,' he assured her quickly as he saw her face. 'It is only a little while since we left. You have forgotten something perhaps?'

She had not. She knew that and her hand trembled as she picked up the telephone at the desk.

'Julia?' It was Maryse, her voice agitated. 'Julia, you must come back at once. Justine cannot speak. She is panicking, almost hysterical. Luc arrived but he cannot do anything. We told him that you had gone and he said to phone the airport and stop you. You must come back, Julia! Luc says that there is nobody to help but you!'

She told Philippe and her eyes lost their sorrow as she noticed his expression. He was struggling between anxiety and glee. Like Luc, he clearly thought that her constant presence would keep Justine normal, and like Luc he disregarded her feelings.

'Will you go back?' he asked, a little more subdued as he saw her stony face.

'Oh, yes! Naturally I'll go back!' she said sharply. 'This time though, Mademoiselle Justine will have some explaining to do!'

'But she is clearly ill!' Philippe said in a rather shocked voice, his eyes on her severe face.

'I think not!' was all that Julia said as they left the building and went back to the car. She would be most surprised to find Justine in anything but blooming health. This was deliberate, a decision to be silent. Before there had been trauma behind Justine's tight face and closed lips, but now there was only a grim determination to hang on to her friend. Yes, Mademoiselle Justine would have some explaining to do!

CHAPTER TEN

WHEN they returned it was to find Luc's Land Rover parked outside, Julia had expected as much. He would not leave Justine for very long if she was once again in trouble. As Philippe stopped the car Lucille came out anxiously, her face lighting up with relief at the sight of Julia.

'I thought that perhaps we would be too late to catch you,' she explained, her hand clasping Julia's. 'Maryse phoned before she left for work. What are we going to do with the child, Julia? She is in her room and utterly silent.'

'I'll go up to her,' Julia said with a reassuring smile at Lucille. 'Where is Luc?' she asked quietly.

'He is with Justine, but as far as I can tell, she is ignoring him,' Lucille said worriedly.

'Yes, she would be!' Julia strode forward and mounted the stairs, a grim look on her face that boded ill for any interference, and the look was still there as she opened Justine's door.

Luc was sitting by the window and she knew at once that he had observed her arrival. His eyes met hers but she looked away. She had to defend herself against this, against the small child who had worked out a way to pull her back if she tried to leave. She had also to defend herself against heartbreak with Luc.

Justine was in bed and it seemed to Julia that she had not left the bed since this morning. Her face lit up with happiness at the sight of Julia but her expression became wary as Julia regarded her with tightened lips and severe eyes.

She was no friend now as she strode to the bed. She was Sister Redford and nothing more as she took the small wrist and looked at her watch, checking Justine's pulse. She expected to do nothing more than bring the child to her senses with this act that would remind her of the past, and as she expected, the pulse was racing with anxiety.

'Yes,' Julia said quietly. 'I think you should stay in bed, Justine. As you can't speak again it will probably be necessary to get you into hospital but of course it will have to be in France. You would not be allowed to be in hospital twice in England. I'll try to get it arranged before I go home.'

'You will still go? You will leave me?' Justine asked quickly and Julia heard Luc's sigh of exasperation. She had been well aware that he had been shocked by her hard attitude, but as Justine spoke so readily he probably understood his niece more than ever.

'Yes, I'll go!' Julia said briskly. 'I have other little girls who need me. You haven't really needed me for a long time, Justine, but I did think that I was a friend!'

'You are my friend, my very best friend!' Justine cried, struggling up in bed, and Julia helped her out, sitting her then on her lap and looking at her with reproof.

'And yet you didn't hesitate to worry me, to worry Uncle Luc, *Grand-mère* Lucille, Maryse and Philippe. You thought only of yourself and not of all the people who love you.'

'I wanted you to stay,' Justine murmured, her eyes filling with tears.

'But I need to go,' Julia said softly. 'I'm a nurse and now there is nobody here who needs nursing, nobody who really needs me. In England there are many people who need me and no tricks will keep me here. Tricks will only make me unhappy and annoyed. I want to be your friend for ever, Justine, but you must give as well as take.'

Suddenly the little arms were around her neck and Justine was crying softly as Julia hugged her close.

'There, now,' she said quietly. 'I'll stay until tomorrow. Get dressed and come downstairs to tell your grandmother that she is not to worry. Explain it all to her and everything will be all right.'

She kissed the wet little cheek and stood, putting Justine on the bed, her eyes avoiding Luc's. He stayed behind to speak to Justine and when he came out Julia was already downstairs explaining to Lucille and Philippe that there was no cause to worry at all.

'I need to speak to you!' Luc said abruptly, his hand coming to her arm, but when she thought he would lead her to his study, he led her outside straight to the Land Rover, putting her inside without comment and getting in to drive away from the house with no explanation at all.

'I should be back there with Justine. I should be there to get her over this small difficulty!' Julia said tightly, her heart accelerating as fast as the Land Rover as he turned in the direction of his own house.

'She has shown herself capable of dealing very well with grown-ups!' he said grimly. 'The only person who was not completely fooled was you. She may get herself over her own difficulties for an hour or two. My difficulties are concerning me at this moment, and for once in my life I intend to be utterly selfish!'

'Not with me!' Julia snapped out bitterly. 'I'm nothing more than a visitor. I'll stay as Lucille's guest tonight and then I'm going home where I belong!'

'I have not tried to stop you for a long time!' Luc assured her tersely. 'You came all the way back from Marseilles for Justine. Can you not spare a few minutes for me?'

She nodded as he glanced sharply at her but she was tight inside, every nerve on edge. He could very well have spoken to her at the Manade de Michaud if he wished to discuss Justine, so why were they hurtling along to his own property?

No doubt she was about to discover why. There was a determination on Luc's face and she knew better than to defy this vibrantly powerful man. He swung the heavy vehicle into his own driveway and strode round to help her out but he said nothing at all until they were in the salon, the door shut resoundingly behind them, and then he spun round to face her, his eyes intent on hers.

'When I went to the *manade* this morning, you were already gone!' he snapped. 'Without a word, without a backward glance you were leaving me!'

Julia gasped at this astonishing assertion, at his open aggression after last night's violence.

'Leaving you did not come into it!' she assured him furiously. 'I was leaving the Camargue, going home. Tomorrow I shall be doing it again. I came here for Justine and it is Justine who is being left as she doesn't need me any more!'

'Would you normally leave in that manner?' he asked sharply. 'Would you go quickly and secretly without a single goodbye?'

'I understood that we said goodbye last night!' Justine said tightly. 'It seemed to me that we had nothing more to say to each other. In any case, you were not there.'

'I arrived just after you had gone,' he said in a more subdued voice. 'Minutes later, the house was in an uproar as Justine decided to lose the power of speech. I would have come after you in any case!'

'I would not have come back if I had been already in England!' Julia assured him. 'Justine would have rapidly come to her senses after a very short time.'

'I would not have come for Justine,' he said quietly, staring at her flushed and angry face. 'I would have come for myself!'

'And you would have been wasting your time!' Julia said shakily, not sure now why he wanted her here. 'We have nothing to say to each other after all.'

'Do lovers never quarrel in England?' he asked softly. 'Do they never become wildly, violently jealous as I did last night?'

'We—we're not lovers,' Julia told him in a tremulous murmur.

'Only because you do not trust me,' he assured her. 'Only because I have been torn between my duty to you in an alien land and my desire for you. If you had trusted me, we would have been lovers many weeks ago, almost from the first night that you came here to the Camargue.'

'You have no right to speak like this!' Julia said shakily, her eyes downcast in case she met his burning gaze.

'It is not a right, *chérie*,' he said softly. 'It is a need. I know that you want me. If you want me enough then I intend to put an end to this discussion as to whether or not we are lovers.' She looked up with wide, startled eyes, the endearment ringing like music in her ears, and his eyes held hers, his proud looks gone as he watched her almost humbly.

'I love you, Julia,' he said simply.

She could not utter a word. For a few seconds she was as silent as Justine had pretended to be this morning but he seemed to understand and he smiled at her, still doing nothing to close the distance between them.

'Lucille told me what Justine had said, what she had imagined, and she told me how you had answered. You said that I was honourable and wonderful and that Justine must not tell me and hurt me. If you believed that when you said it, then how can you doubt me when I tell you that I love you, that there is not and never will be anyone else for me?'

'I—I thought that Rosanne...' Julia's blue eyes could not leave his. 'I didn't want to be hurt again.'

'You will never be hurt, *chérie*,' he promised softly, 'not even one golden hair of your head.'

For a second he just looked at her, and then he opened his arms and Julia ran forward to be collected and held close to his heart. He buried his face in her hair, a shudder racing over him like a sigh of relief.

'Last night,' he confessed, 'I was wild with rage, seeing you in another man's arms, willingly accepting his kisses.'

'I—I wasn't. I couldn't fight him, he was too strong. He just suddenly appeared.'

'And you had no idea that he was here in the Camargue?' he persisted, lifting his head, his dark eyes probing and brilliant.

'Last night, no,' she said truthfully. 'I saw him yesterday earlier when we went to look at the arena but—but strangely enough, I'd forgotten all about him.'

'Why did you not tell me at the time?' he asked softly, still tight with anxiety.

'I didn't want you to know,' she confessed, her head bent to escape from his fierce looks. 'I didn't want anything to happen, anything that would make you angry and spoil...spoil...'

'Spoil what, Julia?' He bent towards her and when she did not answer his strong hand tilted her face. 'Spoil what?' he asked again.

She looked into his eyes, finding her gaze held with no hope of escape.

'I just wanted to be with you,' she whispered. 'Everything seems to go wrong. Everybody needs you.' She suddenly turned her face into his hand, closing her eyes. '*I* need you too, Luc! I need you most of all because everything seems dark when you're not there.'

If she had intended to say anything else, she would not have been able to, because she was wrapped in his arms, his hand in her hair as he caught her to him with a desperate strength that robbed her of breath.

'Then you love me?' he asked urgently.

'I think you know that already,' she whispered. 'I'm not very good at hiding my feelings.'

He smiled slowly, his tight restraint leaving him in one shuddering sigh.

'No, you are not, *chérie*!' he murmured deeply. 'I would not have allowed you to leave me. I would find you if you stepped off the world because I need you too. I need the warmth of you, the peace of you, the golden beauty of you. We will never be parted!'

His lips crushed hers, hurting and fierce before softening to tenderness as he gathered her gently against him.

'You are the bright rays of sunlight, a breath of sanity,' he whispered against her lips. 'I have wanted you since that day when you came so fiercely and proudly into Justine's room to take me to task, that day when later you allowed me to visit even though you were exhausted with your own worries. I have battled against it.' He lifted his head and looked into her entranced face. 'But not very hard,' he admitted with a smile. 'It is too much to battle against the sunlight when all around is darkness.'

Julia stood on tiptoe and did what she had done once before, kissed him softly and sweetly, all her feelings showing on her face. Then it was out of her grasp, the waiting over, joy racing through her and wild excitement as Luc kissed her hungrily, his hands strong and possessive holding her to the fierce demand of his body.

It was enchantment, a sinking, whirling magic that swept her away into light and happiness. His demands did not frighten her. She was shivering with delight, her longing matching his, her kisses wild and hot until he drew back to look at her.

There was a question in his eyes, a burning question that sought an answer, and as her eyes closed and her trembling lips searched again for his, he swept her into his arms, knowing how she felt with no words needed.

It was cool in his bedroom, the open window letting in the light breeze that blew all the way from the sea.

She was glad of the shadowy darkness as he slowly undressed her. Words of protest hovered on her lips, in her mind as he slid away the last concealing garment, but they were never uttered. His head bent, dark and exciting, his lips warm and teasing as they explored the tight, smooth mounds of her breasts, his tongue flicking against the tight peaks until she gasped in shocked excitement.

'Luc!'

'We are just beginning, *chérie*,' he murmured softly. 'I have waited and dreamed of this. Every night when I have taken dinner at the house, I have watched you, wanted you, longed to come later and collect you. Would you have come with me, *ma belle*?' She could only shiver, waves of feeling sweeping over her, and he laughed softly, placing her on the smooth, cool sheets.

'Wait for me now, then,' he said quietly, a vibrancy in his voice that made her mouth dry.

He undressed slowly in the purple darkness of the room, his outline clear but his face not visible, and she thought he was giving her time to change her mind, some inner torment holding him back; but she was too lost to move, her eyes wide in the darkness, her body eagerly waiting to belong to him.

'No!' Her face flushed and her eyes closed as he suddenly flicked on the lamp but his laughter was soft and teasing.

'Yes, my lovely Julia!' he said insistently. 'I have given you the chance to leave me and you have not. Now I wish to look at you.'

His dark eyes moved over her and she knew that he found her beautiful, her eyes closing again at the blaze of passion in his. His hands were heavy and warm on

the flat of her stomach, teasing as they moved to cup
her breasts, and then with a groan he came to her, gathering her against him, his lips claiming hers in a deep,
drugging kiss.

'Lie still!' he ordered as his fingers against her breasts
brought a great spasm of desire that had her arching to
him. 'I want to love you until you are desperate for me,
until you forget that there is anyone else in this world!'

His mouth covered her cries and in spite of his
command, she moved wildly against him, aching for him,
forgetful of her own inexperience.

He forced the upward curve of her body against his,
his breathing heavy as his hand slid to touch her more
intimately, and her melting response drove him to the
end of his control as he lifted her to his hard, demanding body.

'*Please*, Luc!' she pleaded and his response was wild.

'At last you are saying it for all the reasons I need!'
he said thickly. The sharp burst of pain momentarily
stopped his driving possession but his lips covered hers
until she wound her arms back around his neck, softening into willing submission, and his dark eyes held her
prisoner as he looked down at her for a long moment,
searching her flushed face, her innocent blue eyes.

'Beautiful girl,' he murmured softly, the passion
flaring back into his face. 'Crazy, beautiful girl!'

His lips claimed hers again and his lovemaking was
slow and gentle until she moved against him urgently,
her arms tightening, driving him to a wild demand that
could not be controlled, his hoarse cry of pleasure
blending with her moan of delight as at last release came.

'Let me hold you,' he said later when his breathing
had steadied and she lay beside him. His voice was soft

and tender and she dared to look up into his eyes, eyes that were smiling down at her.

'I've never...' she began in blushing confusion and his smile widened as he bent to nip lightly at her skin.

'It is too late to tell me now, *chérie*,' he said with a quiet relish that had her blushes growing. 'In my mind, I have owned you for a long time. It is only the fulfilment of my dreams. Soon we must go back, but for now I will hold you and beg forgiveness for hurting you.'

'You didn't, not really!' she said quickly, but his low growl of laughter and his encircling arms silenced her as she hid her head against his shoulder and gave herself up to the bliss of her happiness. She belonged to Luc and in her heart she knew it was for ever because it had to be.

Later, as she lay in his arms, warm and contented in the lamplit bedroom, the curtains closed against the gathering darkness, the heavy front door shutting out the gloom, she stroked the face that was dearest to her in the whole world. In her arms, the harshness had left his face, the lines of strain had eased away and he turned his head to gaze at her with adoration.

'I thought you intended to marry Rosanne,' she said softly, even now afraid to lose him, and he looked down at her, his frown swift but soon gone.

'Why should I wish to marry a wilful girl when I can have a warm and willing woman?' he asked arrogantly. He relented as he saw her face cloud. 'If I caused you jealousy and pain then I regret it,' he said softly. 'I have known Rosanne since she was a child and I suppose that we have all indulged her. She is possessive and swings wildly from Philippe to me; it just happens to be my turn.'

'Do you think that Philippe...?' Julia began thoughtfully but Luc laughed delightedly and shook his head.

'No, I do not think that Philippe...!' he said amusedly. 'She is spoiled and not at all suitable, apart from the fact that he does not love her. If he even thought of it, I would try my best to dissuade him, as I tried to dissuade Jules,' he finished somberly.

'What about the land that Philippe says you need?' she asked quickly, anxious to get away from Deirdre and the painfully legacy she had left behind.

'He has been telling you a great deal!' Luc said mockingly. 'However he does not know all my plans. The Dupins are seriously thinking of moving north. Rosanne is an only child and she would never manage the *manade* alone, in spite of her riding skills and her knowledge of the stock. She would be better with her inheritance in something a little more easily controlled. When they leave, I have arranged to buy their property and land. It will add to ours and give Justine a separate inheritance.'

'Luc, when—when we're married...'

'And we will be married!' he said fiercely, turning her into the tight circle of his arms. 'I will not let you out of my sight again!'

'When we're married,' she continued carefully, 'would you like to adopt Justine?'

For a second his proud face darkened but then he drew her tightly to him, his breath a sigh against her hair.

'Is there anything in this world that you would *not* do for me, sweetest Julia?' he asked tenderly.

'It would be no sacrifice,' she assured him hurriedly. 'I love her too!'

'And so do many other people,' he said, drawing back to smile down into her eyes. 'There is Lucille who would be lost without her, there is Maryse and there is Philippe who spoils her disgracefully. There are also the gypsies whom she erroneously imagines are her family and now that she is well she will return to her school and her own friends. Life will be happy for her. I am, in any case, her legal guardian, that was in Jules' will. No, my love. I would not like to adopt my niece.' He moved until he was once again lying over her, cupping her face in his warm hands. 'I would like children of my own though, children with eyes as blue as a June sky, with hair like the sunlight.'

'Oh no, Luc!' she protested. 'They'll be dark and fierce like you!'

'And they will kneel at your feet, worship your sweetness, your kindness and your beauty, as I do,' he smiled. 'This land will be theirs and they will be surrounded by a loving family, with a famous grandfather in England.'

'I'll have to go back to tell him,' Julia said quickly, her eyes darting to his face.

'We will go together,' he assured her, 'and then the others will join us for the wedding. Maryse then can take a look at your father's hospital and see if she really wants to follow in your footsteps, although I strongly suspect that she is merely hypnotised by your importance.'

'I'm not important!' Julia began in exasperation but he smiled mockingly and then his teasing ended on a sharp sigh.

'To me, you are everything!' he whispered as his lips closed over hers.

*　*　*

It was the day of the *abrivado* and Julia sat beside her husband watching the *razeteurs* as they defied danger to collect the rosettes from the bulls. This time, Luc had not ridden in the *abrivado*. He had stayed with the others, keeping Julia to the safety of the terrace of the hotel, his arm around her, his dark eyes watchful for any danger as she cradled his son against her.

Now, she looked with contentment at the scene around her. It was her land and they were her people. Lucille sat with pride, nursing Luc's child, friends and admiring relatives around her as they watched the small and beautiful baby with hair like jet and astonishingly blue eyes.

Julia wished that her father could have stayed for this day but he had an important conference in Paris and he had left the day before. Next year, though, he had promised to be here. Justine had forced the promise from him, and in any case he spent a great deal of time visiting them. Maryse was in England, her nursing duties keeping her away, and Luc was satisfied that at Paul Redford's home she was safe and well chaperoned.

'*Dieu!* Look! That one is as fierce and strong as Tamerline!' Luc said to Philippe, leaning forward to watch the bull who had sent the young men racing for the edge of the ring more than once.

'Not surprising!' Philippe growled. 'Tamerline had the same sire, as you know.'

'I wonder if...' Luc began softly but Julia's hand came immediately to his arm.

'You are not going down into that arena!' she said determinedly and Philippe gave a growl of laughter as Luc shrugged and leaned back, tipping his hat forward against the sun.

'Neither are you!' Julia added firmly, her eyes on Philippe.

Luc smiled slowly, his eyes darting sideways to his brother.

'In England,' he said drily, 'it is called being "henpecked", I believe!'

'You seem to thrive on it!' Philippe returned caustically, and Luc's low laugh, never far away nowadays, brought a blush to Julia's cheeks.

'It has its compensations,' he said quietly, his hand capturing hers and lifting it to his lips.

He looked across at Lucille and the small burden she held so proudly. His eyes filled with the same awe that had been in them when he had first seen his son. The blue eyes stared straight at him and then closed sleepily.

'This son of ours is wise as well as beautiful,' Luc said softly. 'He sleeps so much and leaves his mother plenty of time to be with me.'

'Are we staying to the dance?' Julia asked, not caring whether they did or not, and Luc's eyes held hers for a moment.

'I had thought that we would go home, *chérie*,' he murmured, and Julia nodded her agreement as his hand tightened over hers.

The loneliness had passed, the darkness was gone for ever. Now there was only the timeless, mysterious land of sky and water, the fierce black bulls, the wild white horses, and Luc, Luc who never tired of loving her, who filled her days with happiness.

She gave a small, contented sigh, leaning her head against his shoulder, and his free hand came to stroke her face.

'Later, my love,' he promised softly. 'Later.'

Have You Ever Wondered If You Could Write A Harlequin Novel?

Here's great news—Harlequin is offering a series of cassette tapes to help you do just that. Written by Harlequin editors, these tapes give practical advice on how to make your characters—and your story—come alive. There's a tape for each contemporary romance series Harlequin publishes.

Mail order only

All sales final
